Henry Scott Vince

Two Pardons

Vol. II

Henry Scott Vince

Two Pardons
Vol. II

ISBN/EAN: 9783337045074

Printed in Europe, USA, Canada, Australia, Japan

Cover: Foto ©Andreas Hilbeck / pixelio.de

More available books at **www.hansebooks.com**

A Novel.

BY

HENRY SCOTT VINCE.

IN THREE VOLUMES.

VOL. II.

London:

WARD AND DOWNEY,

12, YORK STREET, COVENT GARDEN, W.C.

1889.

PRINTED BY
KELLY AND CO., MIDDLE MILL, KINGSTON-ON-THAMES;
AND GATE STREET. LINCOLN'S INN FIELDS. W.C.

CONTENTS.

TWO PARDONS.

CHAPTER I.

THE ELECTION.

THE important day arrived at last. The nomination of candidates had but whetted the appetites of the country-side politicians, and they now made ready for the substantial dish of the contest. Old elections are gone in the Limbo of Days and Things, and our modern ones have assumed a gravity and dignity much at variance with the stormy saturnalia of by-gone struggles. For in truth, although men of our land may turn with pride to the records of our Parliaments and the wisdom of our states-men, for at least a hundred years our country was in a sad condition whilst they were being elected, when every place that was not led by its owner to elect whomsoever he would (till even a black footman was threatened as an alter-native to some temporarily stubborn borough,

and would have been returned had he been sent)
was a scene of riot and confusion that would
have put old Rome to the blush.   It speaks
volumes for our old statesmen that, with such
material as they got sent to Parliament in those
days, they kept the good ship Britannia on her
course at all.   And certain it is that those who
were seeking the suffrages of the electors paid
dearly for their victories or defeats, not in
money alone, but in dignity.   To be for a fort-
night at once the host and the butt of all the
greasy vagabonds of the town, to be cap in
hand and hand in fist with men from whom
at ordinary times the width of the street was
scarcely division enough, to fawn on men
whose usual habits were to fawn, to put up with
the arrogance of a term, the importance of an
occasion, the haughtiness of an hour—and there
is no such arrogance, no such importance, no
such haughtiness, as that of your Jack in
office, your political pork-butcher, your vintner
with a vote—this was the way in which the
candidate earned his victory, if he gained it,
and with this was his defeat embittered ten-
fold when he lost the day.   And after all this
humiliation and unbending, the candidate faced
on the day of the election about as much

actual danger as the leader of a cutting-out expedition in a foreign harbour, and had doubly to bend, first to the plaudits of his friends, and next from the missiles of his foes.

Add to this the knowledge that the mob were, in those days at least, totally without influence over the election, that the noisy, unwashed, vicious crowd which made the town hideous for a day had not a single vote to the hundred of them. No, their suasion was that of force, the argument of the bludgeon, the logic of the boot ; and it was with very small satisfaction indeed that the good people of Avonham saw that from early dawn there poured into the town all the loafers and roughs from the country round, eager for sport, as they termed the day's proceedings, and, like all bucolic roughs, ready in a moment to exchange the stolid bovine indifference of every-day life for the cruelly unreasoning bovine madness which, when it does break out— which, thank God, happens but seldom—leaves far behind in its vicious destructiveness the hunger-spurred vengeance of the Lancashire meal mob or the cowardly brutality of the race-course rough. Riot is short and sharp in the North, desperate for an hour and then invisible for a year, but though the West rises but seldom, when it does rise it means blood—from both sides too. The Western man will take his opponent's by "fair fighting and no knives," and grudges not his own, fights best indeed when a little is let out ; your ordinary mob has no taste for defeat, and none but Western men will stand against troops.

There was no election in Dunstalne. Their business was done on nomination day, and the former member had a walk over, but he had not omitted to range himself on Mr. Boldham's side at Avonham, and was here to-day with many of his prominent supporters to help the cause and strengthen the hands of his party. Of course, the Dunstalne folk were here in force ; they had had no fun in their own town, it was obvious that they must patronise the entertainment provided for them by their neighbours, and as it would be unfair to come without some addition to the performance, they brought over with them a powerful but roughly-trained brass band, which stationed itself outside the " Woolpack " at seven o'clock in the morning, and raised the hair from the scalps of early breakfasters by its first terrible blast. Forth sallied at once the members of the two bands already engaged by the rival candidates, and, in ten minutes more, quietness and peace were gone, at least for that day, from the town. In half-an-hour the early breakfasters were out in the streets, and the late ones were eating in Pandemonium. The polls were opened at eight. The Mayor was in his place as returning officer, and already the public-houses began to be patronised. The quieter portion of the electors hastened to place their votes on record, and the fray fairly began.

Of course for such a small town as Avonham there was but one polling place needed, and this was a wooden erection covered by a sloping board roof, and approached by steps ; up these the electors climbed and recorded their votes aloud for either candidate. Behind the returning officer were the friends of the two opponents, and from time to time during the day the principals themselves looked in to see how the parties were getting on ; saluting one another courteously when they met, partly from the innate respect each felt for the other, and partly with a view of setting a good example to the two mobs who, as the hour of noon approached, began to get very noisy, and

hailed with tumultuous enthusiasm the various
states of the poll as exhibited from the balcony
of the "George" and the window of the
"Woolpack." These were received from the
checking clerks, who, posted behind the
returning officer, scored each vote as it was
given, and vociferously aided their party by
shouting: "Thank you for Mr. Boldham,"
"Thank you for Sir Headingly Cann." These
gentlemen got hotter and louder and more
enthusiastic as the day advanced—munched at
sandwiches, quaffed bottled ale and sherry
provided by the candidates, and felt greatly
uplifted by being part and parcel of the election
itself, and second in importance only to the
two combatants themselves. Two hours after
the poll opened the first announcement of
numbers was made—

Boldham 97
Cann......................... 89

This was received by the Dunstalne contingent
and the Yellow party with great cheering,
replied to by the Blues with equal vigour.
Then an hour after came the second list—

Boldham 173
Cann 166

—after which Sir Headingly took a drive through the town and gave his followers heart. There was as yet, however, comparatively little excitement, and beyond being made the peg on which to hang cheers and chaff, the figures roused but little real interest. Walter Rivers was, however, busy, and had promised his uncle that he should be ahead at noon. He accordingly marched down from the "George" a large number of voters, and although the movement was vigorously responded to by the opposite party, he was able to keep his word, and shortly after twelve o'clock the Baronet was received at his committee-rooms with a hearty burst of cheers, and saw to his great delight that he had headed his opponent, the numbers shown being—

Cann 246
Boldham..................... 231

Of course the change of affairs gave new zest to the struggle. The voters from the villages immediately in the neighbourhood began to come in. From twelve till two would be the busiest part of the election, and both sides girded up their loins for the encounter. Mr.

Daniel Follwell, an ardent supporter of Mr. Boldham, escorted his own workmen to the poll, and having seen that each man registered for his candidate, he recorded his own vote, and gave his men holiday for the rest of the day. Most of the small shopkeepers followed his example, not only as to holiday, but as to voting, for the influence of the Bank was great, and none dared go against his own interest so far as to run counter to a moneyed man who had the voter in his power. It was greatly on this that Mr. Boldham and Shelman relied for their success. Mr. Rann had spoken truly when he said that politics in Avonham had been dead so long that interest would greatly influence the result of the election ; and Sir Headingly felt somewhat this way himself, for he said to his nephew as they took a glass of sherry together in the middle of the day, "We're beginning to find the Bank influence now, Walter."

"We hold them safe, sir," replied Walter, "though the fight will be closer than I thought at first ; but I am sure of a hundred majority —I have very nearly that on the books. In another election they wouldn't do so well as they are doing now. Besides, we are fighting two towns. Look at Wilmslow (the member for Dunstalne) haranguing away there opposite the 'Woolpack.' "

" He has greatly influenced the villages between here and Dunstalne. I'm afraid we did not look them up enough."

" We shall soon see their effect. They will all be polled by two o'clock. We're in the thick of it now, uncle."

" Yes," said the old man with a nervous laugh, " we're in for it now."

" Yes, and we shall win, and win easily too," said Walter.

" I hope so."

" I am sure of it, uncle. Boldham can't get a majority without bribery, and both he and Shelman know that that won't pay. Come in there ! Who's there ? "

The door opened, and a head was slowly put into the room. The eyes in the head looked inquiringly at the two gentlemen, and the mouth emitted a slight cough.

" Come in, man," said Rivers impatiently. " Now, Hackett, what do you want ? Out with it ! "

Mr. Bill Hackett, the husband of the char-woman before mentioned, shambled slowly into the room and began twisting his rough mole-skin cap nervously round and round in his fingers.

"Now then, Hackett," said Walter, signing to his uncle to leave the conversation in his hands, "what can we do for you?"

"Well, gen'l'men boath," said Mr. Bill Hackett, who eked out the earnings of his better half—of whom he stood in mortal dread —by a little poaching, a little fowl breeding, a little gardening, a trifle of petty larceny, and an infinitesimal modicum of honest work, "I be onwillin' to ent'rupt you when you'm so busy, on'y you see, gen'l'men," he added with a writhe in Sir Headingly's direction, "I be a pore man I be, amazin' pore man I be for sure."

"That's your own fault for not working, my man," said Walter, "and I don't see what it has to do with us either."

Mr. William Hackett looked sheepish and puzzled.

"There's a main lot o' us pore chaps about, gen'l'men," he said. "'Tes surely hard if the gentlevoak can't gie 'un a tarn when they do want 'un like."

"What do you mean, sir?" said Sir

Headingly with much stateliness. It was bad enough to have been worried by this sort of voter in public, but to be intruded upon now and patronised by this fellow was too much.

"What du I mean, zur?" said Hackett. "Whoy, what I mean is this here—what's the use o' my vote to me, Zur 'Edin'ley? I can't eat 'un, can I? I can't drenk 'un, can I? Thick 'ere 'lection 'baint a gooin' on right way noohows as I can zee," he said, raising his voice a little.

"Do you mean to stand there and tell me," broke in Sir Headingly—"to tell me, you—you—you vagabond——"

"Now lookee 'ere, Zur 'Edin'ley, vair words, zur, vair words. I'm a 'lector, I am. I a got my little bit o' vreehold as my vather left I jest so much as you've a got your big vreehold. D'ye zee that, zur?—vair words vor I, zur—I'm a 'lector, I am."

"Now just you listen to me, Mr. Hackett," said Walter, again motioning to his uncle to leave the man to him. "I think I can understand what you want."

"'Tes likely, Muster Rivers, 'tes likely," said the man, with a grin.

" How many voters have you brought round here with you on this errand ? "

The man hesitated.

" Come, don't waste my time. How many fellows did you leave at the bar downstairs ? Tom Purcell was one, wasn't he ? "

" Ees, zur, 'a wur."

" Of course he was, and Edwardes, of Springhill, and his son-in-law Mackerey make three. Now who else was there ?—come, out with it ! "

Mr. Hackett, freeholder and elector, seemed rather cowed by the younger man's bolder way of taking up the running, and answered, rather sheepishly :

" Well, Muster Rivers, there's them three, an' me an' Bill Whiston, him as married my niece, and Jack Onslow, my missuses' brother-law, him as had her sester s'naa, an' we all come in town together, us zix, an' there's Joe White downstairs 'long wi' 'em, as ain't a voted neither not yet. That's all, zur ! "

" Oh, that's all, is it ? Well, that isn't much ; stop a minute till I put their names down, and yours at the head of them."

" My dear Walter," began Sir Headingly, in a hoarse whisper.

Walter answered rapidly in French, which was not among the " 'lector's " accomplishments :

" Let me manage this man, uncle—don't you bother ; he will get nothing from me."

" Now, Mr. Hackett," he went on, " I've got all these names down, and I make seven of them ; what's the next thing ? "

" Well, zur," said the poacher, brightening up as he fancied he spied his expected reward, " the question be just thick-here-a-way, zur. Be they there votes any good to you, gen'l'men, or baint they ? "

" That's the question, as you say ; well, suppose they're not, what then ? "

" Spoasin' they'm *not*, did you zay, Muster Rivers ? " said Hackett, wonderingly.

" Yes, that's what I said ; you can have it the other way about, if you like—you can either suppose they are some good to us or no good to us, just which you please."

" Well, then, zur, I'll miake zo bold as to goo fur to say as how they *be* zum good to 'ee."

" Go on ! "

" Well," said Bill Hackett, in a deeply injured tone ; " sure-*ly*, Muster Rivers, you don't want I to zay no moor ? "

" Oh, no, you might have stopped some time ago, if you pleased."

" Well, then, come, zur," said the fellow, with a sudden burst, " me an' my mates is ready to goo and vote right straight vor Zur 'Edin'ly, see now."

" Well, why don't you go ? "

" But, Muster Rivers, baint we to get nothin' for all these 'ere votes—why, look, see there's zeven on 'em."

" How much do you want, Hackett ? "

" Well, zur, I reckon as they'm wuth a vive pound a-piece to me for a-gettin' on 'em for 'ee—there now ! "

" And that is what you want ?—five times seven, that makes thirty-five. I suppose you want five pounds for your own vote ? "

Mr. William Hackett fairly laughed with glee at his success. What a simple thing it had been to manage " the gentlevoak," and how easy it was to get favours from them at " 'lection time "—why wasn't there a 'lection every year instead of once in eighteen ? He rubbed his hands, and answered the little query with a chuckle.

" Well, I spoase zo, zur."

" Well now, Hackett," said Rivers, rising,

and placing one foot on the chair, and pointing one finger airily at the chuckler, "just you listen to me a minute."

"Cer'nly, zur."

"You've come here to-day with your precious seven votes and you expect us to give you thirty-five pounds for them——"

There was an unpromising tone to these words, so Hackett listened open-mouthed and very open-eared, and made no reply.

"Now you can just turn round and walk straight out of that door, for you won't get one farthing."

Mr. Hackett's fingers lost their hold of the moleskin cap, and it fell to the floor.

"And, another thing I'll tell you, now you're here. You'll go straight to the other side and make your offer there; try it on— you'll find when you do come to vote that you are marked men; the other side won't have you, for I shall see Mr. Boldham's agent at once and tell him of your offer, or at least my uncle will—you've made the offer to him, and I witness it. Boldham's man will be afraid to poll you, for he knows that if you vote for him we shall be down on them for bribery, and win or lose, they get the worst of that. Try it and see. How much are the seven votes worth now, eh ? "

Mr. Hackett much chapfallen here.

" And how much is your personal liberty worth ? Do you know what you've been doing by offering to sell votes ? "

Mr. Hackett, much chapfallen still, gasped out a negative.

" You don't ; go and ask a lawyer then, or wait till the assizes, for we shall prosecute you and your mates for doing it, and you'll find out then—you especially. Now you can walk and tell your friends how nicely you've managed for them. Come—pick up your cap and march ! "

A more deeply disgusted elector than Mr. William Hackett, freeholder, has never gone out of a committee-room, and never gone out with a more woe-begone and forlorn appearance.

Sir Headingly turned to his nephew with an air of relief.

" Well, you certainly managed that fellow remarkably well ; I was really half afraid at one time, Walter, that you were actually going to treat with him. I wouldn't have missed the vagabond's discomfiture for the world ; of course, you intend to tell Boldham's man ? "

" My dear uncle, I am in hopes that there will be no need for doing so ; if I am not very much mistaken, Hackett's terror, which I flatter myself was genuine, will communicate itself to his comrades, unless some Dunstalne man gets hold of him first, and that's not very likely in this house, and we shall have a deputation of them here presently begging for mercy and promising to vote for us. Hark, I can hear someone stumbling up the stairs now——Come in ! "

Two of the companions of the discomfited Bill Hackett appeared at the door and looked pleadingly at Sir Headingly.

" What is it, my men ? " said that worthy.

" Whoy," said the elder man Edwardes, and then he nudged his son-in-law, and remained silent.

" Whoy," said Mackercy, and also spake no more.

" You've come to ask for fifty pounds instead of the thirty-five that your precious friend Hackett wanted, I suppose," said Rivers.

" No-a, zur, us baint," said Edwardes, in a kind of mild despair, " doan't 'ee goo for to mex us up along o' he, Muster Rivers, 'twertn't noo vault o' ourn, zur."

" Well, what do you want to say ; are you going to vote for us, or against us ? Now, come—sharp—out with it—do you think I've got nothing to do but talk to you all day ? "

" We coom in town s'marning," said the younger man, elbowing himself past his father-in-law, and standing sheepishly in front of him, " fur to vote fur you, zur ; well, on th' road we meets Bill Hackett, an' he says as how we got to zee you 'fore we goos to vote. Well, zur, he do leave we downstairs, and when he do come back, he do tell we as how you be goin' to gie we all up to jail for hee's vault ; well, us baint goin' fur to ha' that, zur, zoo we'en come up here fur to tell 'ee as we be goin' right away fur to gie 'ee our voates, and then we be goin' whoam like ; good marnin' to 'ee. gen'l'men," added Mackerey, hurriedly backing past his father-in-law, " an' good luck to 'ee. doan't 'ee goo fur to be hard wi' Bill Hackett. gen'l'men, he be a poor mackey moon, zir, and I do think he've a got beer a'ready this marning. Good marning, gen'l'men. Come on, you ; " and clutching the arm of his father-in-law, who was overpowered with respect at the clever way in which his son-in-law had extricated the party, he left the room, and Walter and the Baronet were again left alone.

Walter laughed quietly.

" I'll see that those seven votes are registered, they may be useful ; here is the latest state of the poll coming, uncle ; you must go out on to the balcony and say a few words ; well, Simmonds " (to a young man, who entered, bearing a paper), " what news now ? "

" Still ahead, sir ; still ahead, Sir Headingly. Here are the figures, sir. They're pretty correct. I've kept a careful check over the registering clerks, and I think you will find this right."

The new record showed that Sir Headingly's position was still better than it had been at noon. The numbers now were—

Cann........................ 406
Boldham..................... 323

Ringing cheers greeted this announcement when it was displayed from the balcony, and Sir Headingly, in response to the calls of his followers, stepped out and made a short speech. The old man's mettle was up, and he was elated with his success.

As he and Walter drove up the street to the

hustings they saw Mr. William Hackett and his fellow-electors standing at the polling place and recording their votes. The clerks were shouting " Thank you for Sir Headingly Cann " as each one gave in his adherence to the winning candidate, but the voters seemed as though they were not combining pleasure with their duty.

" We get those votes, thanks to your cleverness," said the Baronet, looking gratefully at his nephew.

" Oh, no, uncle ; it was Bryceson who put me up to that trick. You must thank him when you see him. He was the man who gave me that idea, and a capital one it was for us. Look at that fellow Hackett's face."

And, indeed, Mr. Hackett went home to his better half in such a desponding, disgusted, and petulant humour that she was compelled to break a stave of a butter tub over his devoted head before she could restore him to anything like himself ; and when she heard the result, the barren result, of his negotiations with the only candidate he had dared to interview, she fell into so great a passion, and made such determined preparations for breaking the rest of the tub in the same manner, that the foiled elector quitted his freehold in undignified haste, and sought to dispel his chagrin and disappointment by a course of strong liquors and smoke.

Meanwhile the hopes of the Yellow party declined as those of the Baronet's rose. At two o'clock the numbers were again exhibited, and again the Blue candidate was seen to be more than holding his own. Good fight as Mr. Boldham was making, he had great odds against him—the odds of prejudice and unwillingness to bring about change, and well liked as he himself was in the town, the personal popularity of the Baronet was against him as well. The state of the poll at two o'clock was—

Cann 534
Boldham 410

"Well, Wilmslow," said Mr. Boldham, cheerfully, as they met in the private room at the "Woolpack," where they were joined by Shelman, who looked as amiable as usual, "we seem to be out of it, eh? The old influence too much for us, I expect."

"We have made a capital fight, for a first struggle. You will have five hundred votes, and that is wonderful for a little place that has for forty years been represented by the other party, and has gone eighteen years without a contest at all. I feel much encouraged, and I am sure you will receive the congratulations of the party on your gallant battle."

" Well, well, we mustn't despair. As you say, we have stirred up the other people a bit, and they must know now that they can't expect always to have matters their own way."

" We must have an Association as soon as this is over," said Shelman.

" Do you think Cann's people are better organised than ours ? " enquired the member for Dunstalne.

" Oh dear no," replied Shelman, " they never dreamed of a contest. The news was like a thunderbolt in the market-place. We posted our bills at night, you know, and next morning we were canvassing. Oh, no, we had rather the start of them, in fact. Rivers has worked well, of course."

" But not better, I am sure, than you have, Mr. Shelman. I must felicitate you on your first effort as an electioneering agent."

Shelman bowed.

" The town seems quiet, that's one thing I'm very glad of," said Boldham.

" It won't be very quiet after four o'clock," said Shelman, sharply. " There are a lot of quarrymen in town, and they're drinking pretty freely, and so are most of the country people. The roughs about here, too, have got the idea into their heads that there would be plenty of occupation and heaps of money for all of them if the railway came here, and that Cann is trying to keep it away ; and I shouldn't wonder if they let him know it before the day is out."

Mr. Boldham looked grave. " I trust not," he said. " I should be very grieved if there were any violent scenes in the town after the poll is closed."

" Well, we must hope for the best," said Shelman, carelessly. " Now, uncle, I am going round to the polling place again, and I shan't return here till after four o'clock."

Shelman did not remain long at the polling place ; he set off up the town in a few minutes, and visited several of the houses. He had a short interview with Messrs. Jack Onslow and Bill Whiston, two worthy members of the family of the henpecked Bill Hackett. These two gentlemen had imbibed just enough to make them extremely cross with their disappointment, and to have disarmed them of any caution. He listened to their tale and then condoled with them, recommended them not to go home yet, but to wait till the evening, and assured them that they had been shamefully treated.

A little after three o'clock he mounted his horse, which was kept saddled and ready for him at the "Woolpack," and rode again to the market-place. The town was getting a little tired of this election plaything, and the hoisting of the last hour's numbers only partially aroused the crowd; they were—

Cann......................... 597
Boldham..................... 459

There was some cheering as Shelman rode up, and just at this time a large number of voters were registering. All who had not yet done so were pressing up to the poll, and the agents were very sharply watching for any last great move on the part of the enemy. For the first time in the day Rivers and Shelman met. They raised their hats to each

other at first and then shook hands, at which
the friends of both parties cheered and commented in various ways on the incident.

" That's right," shouted one. " Let 'un
shake hands afore they do vight."

" We'll put thee up next time, Muster
Shelman," cried another, and the Yellows
cheered.

" So 'ee may," roared a brazen-lunged Blue,
" an' we'll put Muster Rivers whur we be a-
puttin' 's uncle now," which was the signal for
acclamation by the Blue party, and the Blue
song was loudly raised, to be replied to by the
Yellow version, when a line of it had been
sung and roared. The bands blared defiance
at one another, the banners waved and the
crowds hurrahed, as if noise and colour would
yet alter the fortune of the day.

But although the votes of the last hour
were pretty evenly distributed, and although
to make their minority as small and their
defeat as creditable as possible Mr. Boldham
and his lieutenants brought up every available
unit of their forces, it was of no avail. Four
o'clock struck, the Mayor declared the poll
closed, and the election was over. It was not
long before the official report was known, and

Mr. Sennett announced the result of the day's struggle—

Cann 635
Boldham..................... 482

But Avonham's troubles were not over for that time ; the worst of the day was to come.

CHAPTER II.

THE one inhabitant of Avonham who was devoutly glad that the business of the day was done was the Mayor. He had discharged his duties that day most ably and courteously, and to the satisfaction of everybody connected with the election ; he had been thanked by both the candidates in the set speeches which each had made on the declaration of the result, and he sought his home self-satisfied, but intensely weary ; never was man so glad of slippers and loose coat ; he descended to his cellar for a bottle of his choicest wine, and sat down to his dinner with a feeling of intense gratitude for his deliverance from the turmoil of the day. His meal finished, and the bottle half, or perhaps a little more than half, emptied, Mr. Mayor placed his legs on a chair, carefully adjusted his silk handkerchief over his head, and slept the sleep of the hard-worked just man, after the manner of his forefathers.

Doubtless if he could have removed the roofs of the houses of the burgesses over whom he that year held sway, and peeped, Asmodeus-like, into their rooms, he would have seen many a one just as tired of the affair as he was himself, and seeking to forget the derangement which the town had suffered in very much the same comfortable way as his worship. Had the place been left to its own devices, and had none but the real electors been consulted as to the way in which the rest of the evening should be spent, there would have been little difference between the close of that day and the evening of any great market, and the white boards of the polling booth, and the election posters, still covering the walls in all directions, would have been the sole remaining signs of the bygone contest. Everyone would have gone gravely and peaceably to his business again, one to his farm and another to his merchandise, as the good old Scriptural phrase puts it, and the election would have been comfortably stowed away in people's memories, to serve, perhaps, as a topic of conversation for many a future day, but to trouble the town no more.

It would have been with it as it was periodically with the river ; for eight months in the year the Avon flowed peacefully over its pebbly bed limpid and pure, for three months more it was swifter, deeper, and, as the country-folks called it, "muddly-like," and very often during the one remaining month of the year, or at any rate during a great part of it, the Avon would assert itself, would come plashing and tumbling into the houses in the lower part of the town, driving the inmates to upstairs rooms to be rescued in boats, swimming the family wash-tubs and large crockery merrily round the ground floor, and finally, leaving an inch deep deposit of mud on the boards and the street pavement outside, return to its bed for another eleven months. Nothing was ever done ; the town fathers did not dream of raising the banks and keeping it out, they were perfectly acquainted with its ways and did not heed its winter vagaries ; you see it was their own river and they understood it. So with the election—for eighteen years the tide of events had flowed on peacefully, occasionally local excitement had raised ripples on the stream, and now the election had come, and the tide of events slopped over and flooded the minds of the township, just as the river

flooded its houses. And just as the floods
were forgotten yearly, when the river resumed
its peaceable behaviour, so would the election
have been forgotten if the Avonhamites had
been left to themselves. But there were outside influences at work and pressure from
without, and the town was destined to be
flooded this time in a manner which would
not easily fade out of the memories of its
inhabitants.

The inns, both great and small, were full ;
at the " George " there was jubilation, at the
" Woolpack " irritation, and cogitation at the
" Bear." The Blue party celebrated their
victory by much singing of songs, much
shaking of hands, and draining of glasses and
cans ; the Yellows were no less boisterous,
were, indeed, even louder, but not so hearty ;
and the customers at the " Bear " were noisy,
but only conversationally so. The two parties
met there more ; the ground was neutral and
argument more rife, but the frequenters of
the hotel were of the better class, and whatever discussion went forward was carried on
decorously and without heat. The general
feeling seemed to be that there had been a
much closer contest than was expected, that a

majority of no more than a hundred and fifty-three was calculated to cloud the victory of the Blues with some degree of apprehension for a seat which had been deemed so secure. However, the Blues did not seem cast down, they took their victory as they found it, and were quite satisfied. " So long as they won," their leaders said, " that was enough for them." Mr. Boldham had been the strongest man they would ever have arrayed against them, and no other would have got the votes he did. Meanwhile, in the small inns and beershops, the roughs of the town, the quarry-men from the down, and the Dunstalne mob had collected and were singing, and dancing, and drinking, and fast working themselves up to the point where mischief begins in these matters.

It was about eight o'clock, and still perfectly light, when out of a beershop in the neighbourhood of the canal wharf, the favourite resort of the bargees who worked the fly-boats, which brought Avonham most of its London and Bristol merchandise, came pour-ing a stream of half-tipsy roughs, who made a ring and surrounded a Dunstalne man and an Avonham man, who having differed as to

the number of times Nelson defeated the
" Hemperor Bonyparty," or the age of the
" Duke " (there is but one Duke for West of
England men), were going to settle the matter
in the good old English fashion. Hot and
flushed with drink and excitement they came
rushing out into the open place next the wharf
and watched the varying fortunes of the
struggle, encouraging each his man with loud
shouts, dancing, howling, disputing, but never
interfering with either of the two bruisers who
pummelled away at one another for half-an-
hour until the Dunstalne man yielded and
was led away by his friends, whilst the Avonham hero was seized by his own party, taken
off in triumph to the house where the dispute
had originated, and regaled at the expense of
his admiring townsmen. From that time and
from this slight incident was Avonham's peace
once more taken away. The Dunstalne men
who had come into the town that day were all
on the losing side, the party they had assisted
had been defeated, and the tide of generosity
which would have flowed so freely from win-
ners was trickling from losers much too slowly
and in much too scanty a volume to please the
recipients, who had imagined, the wish being

father to the thought, that they were coming into a land of rejoicing and plenty, where, after assisting in beating the common foe, they would be bountifully regaled at the expense of the "emancipated slaves who had long groaned beneath his yoke," to quote one of their most prominent orators ; but the Yellows in Avonham were not dispensing their favours as conquerors. The Dunstalne men found that the joyful libations of the victors and the despair-begotten draughts of the defeated were different things entirely. It was therefore with a great access of delight that a Dunstalne man who, having met in the street three of his comrades tired and thirsty, had taken them into the " Five Stars " to eat and drink, received in response to his enquiry as to what was to pay, the answer from the usually gruff landlord, " Nothin' t'you, nur noo one else as is on right side."

" Right side's bin wrong side t'day," said an Avonham man sitting near.

" 'Twon't be that thur way long, thoo," replied the Dunstalne man ; " here, coom, drink you, surr, an' let t'other chap drink ; there's nowt to pay, thee sayst, fill another pot, then."

The landlord readily complied.

"Matey," said one Avonham man to another, up street, "dost knoo Sam Willums be gi'en away aal hees beer fur nowt?"

"No!" said the other, galvanised into sudden interest, "whur?"

"Down to 'Vive Stars,' mun; will 'ee coom an' ha' a drop o't?"

"Ah, will I nuther?" said the other, wiping his lips.

But they were disappointed, the landlord was obdurate; they were "dirty Blues," they were informed, and they were expelled with more force than politeness. Rejected in this rough manner, they sought counsel and help of their friends, and, collecting a force of their allies, drove furiously at the "Five Stars;" the windows were broken, the Dunstalne men inside roughly handled, the heads of two of the landlord's barrels staved in, and the landlord himself flung out into the street, whilst the invaders ran riot in his bar and cellar. Bitterly regretting his action in refusing liquor which was so soon to be taken from him, he sought aid of his cronies and of his recently expelled customers, and having been reinforced, made another attack upon his own house and reinstated his free customers at the expense of all his windows and bar-fittings.

This time, however, the combat was carried into the enemy's country, and the Blues were chased down the street, until they reached the shelter of a little house called the "Swan." Alas! this proved the destruction of the "Swan," for although the fugitives managed to make good their escape and flee through the back way, yet the house was given up to the vengeance of their pursuers, the blue flag torn down, the whole of the windows broken, and the bar wrecked; and then the Yellow mob, by this time a hundred strong, and reinforced every minute, paraded the upper side streets of the town, and saluted every Blue house with a volley of stones which went smashing through the windows, scaring the inmates almost to death. Presently, not contented with alarming this portion of the town, they marched in fair order, but with immense noise, into the open space in front of the church, where they halted for a moment as if irresolute, and then raised deafening shouts of defiance of their enemies. In a minute or two they were joined by all of the Yellow party who were ready for mischief, a considerable

20—2

contingent who were of no party at all, but
ripe for any riot, and a sprinkling of Blues,
who discovered, to their great disgust, that
their halloaing and whooping on behalf of
their side had not been so productive of solid
and liquid benefits as they had anticipated at
the commencement of the day ; finding, then,
that nothing was to be gained by peace they
gravitated easily to the riotous faction and
were soon as prominent as any ; it is, perhaps,
unnecessary to say that Mr. Hackett and his
disgusted contingent, having drunk themselves
pot-valiant, were of this party.

Some unconscious road surveyor had aided
the Goddess of Discord, by leaving at the side
of the street three heaps of stones, with which
it was intended to mend the road at the top
of the town. Certain it was that their mis-
sion to-night was not to repair the town ; the
mob armed themselves with the missiles, and
before the affrighted inhabitants had time to
protect their windows with shutters, the crashing of glass and the shrieks of terrified women
proclaimed that the riot was assuming formidable proportions. In five minutes the town
was in a state of panic, and the mob were
masters of the situation.

The Mayor, hastily summoned, showed both
courage and good sense ; he went at once
into the street and endeavoured to reason with
the mob, but his eloquence was vain, he was
driven back to his house, but escaped by his
garden, and making his way to the market-
place, surrounded by a few faithful followers,
there read the Riot Act, that ancient ceremony
which still ranks among our most cherished
and useless remedies against Force. And the
Mayor did better ; he sent his own man on a
good horse to the railway station, at which was
the nearest telegraph office, and despatched a
telegram for troops. All over the town the
householders were barricading their dwellings,
conveying their women and children into the
back rooms, and preparing to make what stand
they could against the mad crew, who were
wrecking the town. There was no time to
swear in special constables ; many of the
rioters were armed in some fashion with staves
and pokers, hatchets and stones, and it would
need a well organised and trained body to
cope with them ; the local police were so few
in number as to be helpless, though they did
their duty well, and so the work of destruction
went on, and the unimpeded ruffians were

going systematically through the town, breaking the windows, and destroying, as far as
they could, all the property of the voters
for Sir Headingly Cann. The "Bear" was
attacked, and though the ex-soldier landlord
fought gallantly for his property and made
two or three of the party wish they had not
joined the fray, he was wounded by a stone
and dragged into his house bleeding and ex-
hausted, only just in time for his servants
to close the ponderous gateway door, which,
being built of massive oak planks and iron
clampings, resisted all efforts to break it down.

Foiled in this attempt, the rioters next
divided themselves into three portions, one
continuing down the main street towards the
bridge, one crossing into the churchyard to
attack the houses beyond, and the third, which
we will follow, to commence the destruction
in South Street. Acting under some instruc-
tions from someone in authority, they passed
Mr. Bompas's house without injury, but
smashed in the panes of the two next to it,
and then, with loud shouts, crossed the road
to the gate of the "Coombes." It was known,
of course, that the proprietor had no vote, but
there seemed to be an understanding that

something special was to be done here, for a louder outcry than had yet been made was raised as they halted before the gate. But here, for the first time, they were confronted and cowed. As Tom Purcell, the leader, a brawny six-foot ruffian, thrust his hand through the gate to get at the lock, he started back with an awful scream of pain and fell fainting into the arms of his nearest follower, his arm broken at the wrist. There was a moment of indecision and then a voice from inside the gate, cried, in deep, firm tones :

"What do you want here, you vagabonds ?"

There was a pause, and a silence, and then someone who had made a strategic movement to the rear on seeing the fate of the unlucky ringleader said, "Look 'ow 'ee've a sarved pore Tom Purcell's arm."

"I'll serve your head the same fashion if you put it this way, young man," said the deep voice again. The figure of the speaker was not seen.

"Break down th' giate," shouted someone (also in the rear).

"Oh ! you want the gate open, do you ?" said the same voice, and the gate swung inwards on its hinges. "Now then !"

A man rushed forward, but in a moment came flying back and crashed down on the pavement as though a horse had kicked him. Next, another peeping in cautiously to see where the owner of this mysterious voice was concealed received a rap on the head which made him doubt for a minute or two whether he had a head left to rap. This was a chilling reception for the crowd, though a very warm one for those who had sampled the fare which the garrison of the "Coombes" was providing for them. Obviously the only thing to do was to let fly at the windows, and not to come to close quarters with those at the gate, so four or five of the fellows drew back to the other side of the street and threw. There was a shiver of glass and a cheer from the crowd. But it was rudely interrupted by a sudden charge from the gate. Galbraith, who now showed himself for the first time, came first, followed by the negro and Bryceson. Dashing at the men nearest to the gate, they struck boldly and fiercely each at his man, and one fellow was seized in the negro's powerful grip, hauled half-way across the road, and flung down into the garden. Then Galbraith and Bryceson retired to the gate and waited for the foe to advance. But the foe had no stomach for the fray. Evidently these were not long-suffering citizens, but dangerous men who meant fighting. There was an undignified scuffle, and a great show of assisting off their wounded, and, with a parting yell, the portion of the rioters who had undertaken the assault of South Street withdrew, taking with them their unfortunate leader with a broken arm, the inquisitive peeper with a "confused" brain pan, and three others with substantial marks and sanguinary proofs of the courage and determination of the garrison. Entirely occupied with their own safety, they forgot all about the unfortunate prisoner, but left him behind in a most uncomfortable position, lying on the gravel path, with the heavy foot of the negro on his chest.

"Pick him up, Ned," said Bryceson, "and take him into the house. We'll see who he is."

The victim was jerked upon his feet, and hustled into the house with a roughness that surprised him and took away all power of resistance even if he had intended any. Ned pushed him along the hall and into a room, where Bryceson and Galbraith followed with a light.

" Now then, turn him round, and let's have a look at him."

Ned twisted the captive round to face the lamp, and there, blinking and shivering with light and fright combined, was Adolphus Carter.

Galbraith looked sternly at him as he crouched under Ned's powerful hand. Then, turning to Bryceson, he said :

" Why, this fellow is one of Mr. Bompas's clerks. What's the history of this ? "

" Ask him," answered Bryceson, laying down his formidable club. " Now then, sonny, speak up ! Give him a shake up, Ned. That's right. Now, then, what were you doing out there wrecking and plundering, eh ? "

Mr. Adolphus had already expended all the stock of courage which he had ever possessed. He burst into tears, and made no answer. The only movement, either, of which he seemed capable was that of flinging himself at the feet of the two friends and grovelling on the carpet before them. They looked at each other for a moment, and burst into a roar of laughter, in which the negro joined.

" Get up, you unhappy little cur," said

Galbraith, contemptuously. "What harm have I ever done you or your ruffians that you should attack my house? Ned and Walter, as the street's clear, just walk over to Mr. Bompas, offer him any assistance, and if you want me fire a shot, and I'll be with you in a brace. If not ask Mr. Bompas to step over here under your escort. I should like him to see this object."

Mr. Bompas had been out to endeavour to assist his friend the Mayor, and by dint of much courage and moral suasion had persuaded some of the crowd to disperse. He had left the Mayor at the Town Hall, and now came down South Street to see what had happened there. The emissaries met him at his own door. He came over at once to the "Coombes."

"Good evening, Mr. Bompas," said Galbraith, as he met them at the open door. "Lively time, for a country town. Just come in here; we've got something belonging to you, I think."

"Something belonging to me, my dear sir?" said Bompas.

"Yes," said Galbraith, ushering him into the room, and pointing to the pale-faced, cringing wretch who was blubbering in the corner. "That thing there's yours, isn't it."

Mr. Bompas held up his hands in astonishment as his articled pupil again flung himself down on his knees before his captors and his master.

"In the name of all that's unfortunate," said Bompas, "what is the meaning of this?"

"This gentleman has turned rioter, it seems, Mr. Bompas, and brought a score or a couple of score vagabonds down the street just now to wreck my house. My friend and I and my servant have made our defence good, and this is a prisoner we took in a sally."

"He was pickin' up a rock," said Ned, "and he's jus' done gone frown one. I picked him up an' toted him in, and thar he is."

"You unhappy boy," said Mr. Bompas, "what induced you to join in this deplorable and ruffianly riot?"

No answer from the weeper.

"How old is this interesting youth?" said Bryceson.

"Between twenty-three and twenty-four, I believe," said Bompas.

"Ye—ye—ye—yes!" sobbed the object.

"Now look here," said Galbraith, sternly.

" Listen to me—get up off that floor, and stop that howling." Carter slowly rose. " Now, you cowardly hound ! who put you up to this outrage on me ? you haven't pluck enough, you miserable cur, to have started it yourself —tell me that, and you shall walk out of this house with your employer, free ; if you don't you shall spend your next night in jail, if I drag you there with my own hands."

Carter looked piteously at his master, but seemed unable to speak ; there was a pause for a moment or two, and then Bompas spoke.

" Was there anyone ? "

" No—no—one put me u—u—p to it," said Carter ; " I di—di—did it my—i—self."

" Whose windows did your blackguards break up street ? " said Bryceson.

" M—i—ister Regler's a—and Mr. Mo— o—dan's."

" Are your windows broken, Mr. Bompas ? "

" No, my dear sir, they are, I am happy to say, intact ; if this misguided young man had any influence over the crowd he may have exerted it for my benefit. Had you any such authority, Carter ? "

" Yes," answered the prisoner.

" And what was the reason for the attack

on Mr. Galbraith ? This is an election riot,
and he has taken no part in the election and
has no vote."

"It was a mi—is—is—take of the mob. I
was try—i—ing to stop them."

"That's a lie," broke in Ned, "you jus'
done frowin' one rock, an' when I pick you up
'n run in de garden wif you you was pickin'
up 'nudder one. You bad scoun'rel—w'at
you wan' int'fere wi' my master fo' ! he nebber
int'fere wi' you, you bad li'l—li'l—li'l—tater-
bug." Ned fished about for this word a few
times and brought it out with a scream that
made Carter jump again.

"Mr. Bompas," said Galbraith, "there's
some mystery in this—this fellow's tale is not
true, and your suggestion as to my having
nothing to do with the election is a very good
one ; he has some motive which I don't
fathom. Where can I put him into a safe jail
for the night—this town's no good ? Ned,
saddle the horses, we'll start at once."

"Mr. Galbraith," said Bompas, "will you
deign to listen to me for a few moments if I
venture to urge something in mitigation of
your suggested plan."

"My dear sir, whatever you say will, I am

sure, from all I've ever seen or heard of you, be straightforward and honourable ; you may speak freely and with authority here, if you choose."

"I thank you, sir ! Gentlemen, I have known the father of this unhappy lad for many years ; he is a clergyman who is known and respected all over Marlshire. The occurrence of to-night, to find his son in this position, would break his heart, and this young man's mother's heart, too. The lad is but young, gentlemen—he may have been led astray—his brain may have been turned by the deplorable turmoil of this hor—ri—ble day, which I wish the town had never seen. Now, if you will consent to release him conditionally on his confessing to me the reasons which actuated him in his insane attempt on your house, I will use all my endeavours to induce him to make them known to me or to his father. My dear Mr. Galbraith, I ask this not as any favour to myself, but in mercy to my two old friends, his father and mother, who would be heart-broken if they knew of their son's wickedness." The good old fellow's voice trembled as he made his appeal. Galbraith was moved by his plea.

" God forbid, Mr. Bompas, that I should add any sorrow to an old man's grey hairs ; let it be as you say, with all my heart ; the vagabond isn't worth the trouble of a good man's help, and perhaps he's not worthy an honest man's enmity. Take my advice, young sir, and go home to your father ; keep out of Avonham for a week or two, I daresay Mr. Bompas will give you a holiday, and keep out of my sight for the rest of the century, if we live so long. Open the door, Ned, and let him go." And Mr. Adolphus Carter, with downcast eyes and abject mien, crawled out of the room.

" Mr. Bompas," said Bryceson, heartily, " you're a brick ! Harry ! Mr. Bompas and the Mayor have been trying to restore order in this place ; if they can get fifty fellows together they can keep the peace—if not, half the town 'll be down ; we must help, too, old boy. We've seen many worse troubles than this, Mr. Bompas. Ned, mix us three stiff horns, and then come out and fight."

Ned grinned at this, and speedily appeared with the desired refreshments.

" We none of us want Dutch courage,

Walter," said Galbraith, smiling, as he took his glass.

"No matter," said the irrepressible Walter, "we shall be none the worse for it any way. Now, Mr. Bompas, we'll see you safe. Come along, Ned."

They left the house perfectly deserted and dark, at which Mr. Bompas made some demur, but was answered that the house might look after itself, and that they were not afraid that, after their first reception, the rioters would return. Mr. Bompas could not but admire the calm and quiet manner and total absence of fear in the young men. They walked swiftly down to the Town Hall, where the Mayor and his followers were.

"Come to reinforce you, Mr. Mayor," said Bryceson.

"I am in hopes they have partially dispersed," said the Mayor.

"Not a bit of it," said someone; "just hark to that row!"

A loud shout resounded up the street.

"They've got to Killett's house," said a young fellow, grasping his heavy stick; "let's go and help him."

"Come along," said Galbraith, and he,

Bryceson, the negro, and half a score young fellows started up the street. As they arrived on the outskirts of the crowd, they perceived that a regular siege was being laid to the ex-Mayor's house; that the besieged and two of his men were holding out stoutly, and that he had just saluted the mob with a pail of scalding water; this at first had provoked a laugh, but the rioters were in an ugly temper, and a quarryman, elbowing his way to the front, shouted to one of his mates:

"Gi' me hold o' thy crowbar, thee fool; doesn't thee see corner stwun o' th' house here? gi' me hold, we'll ha' th' lot deawn in vive minutes."

But as he dealt his third heavy stroke, trying to wedge the point of his crowbar in between the stone and brick work, a heavy cudgel descended on the side of his head, and he fell prone. At the same time a cheer was raised, and the rescue party, attacking the mob in rear, dashed through it, smiting right and left as they passed, and facing them, fairly drove them back. They were at once joined by Killett and his men, who ranged themselves alongside them. The giant forms of the butcher and the negro, and the determined atti-

tude of the rest, made the crowd hesitate for a
moment. Then, a man dashed out at Galbraith,
who was on the right of the party—he had
never made a greater mistake or a worse selection in his life. Before he could strike a blow,
he was seized by the throat, flung down on
the pavement, lifted up and held a moment
over his adversary's head, and then hurled
violently forward on to the heads of some of
the rearmost of the crowd ; a feat like that had
never been seen in Avonham ; she had had her
famous wrestlers, and was the centre of as tall
and stalwart a race as any that lives in England,
but never a man there had seen a show of
strength like that ; even for such a foe there
was for a moment a buzz of applause and a
murmur of commendation that almost drowned
the cries of the crowd. Not a few were the
immediate deserters of the cause. Throwing
stones and breaking Blue windows might be
very good fun, but to be dashed on to a pavement and then sent spinning into the air at
men's heads was a little too cooling for the hot-
test enthusiasm to resist ; and when the little
band, headed by the very man who had shown
twice this night that he would not be attacked
without sharp retaliation, dashed forward with a

21—2

cheer into the front ranks of the crowd, and by dint of sheer strength drove them back across the road, half the fellows felt the game was getting too exciting, and fled. The rest of the combat was short, sharp and decisive. Twenty people, who had only before wanted leaders to attack the rioters, now joined the fray, and in a few minutes the largest of the three crowds, which were doing so much damage to the town, was dispersed. As they straggled past the Town Hall, pursuers and pursued mixed up together, the loud voice of the Mayor was heard proclaiming that he had sent for troops, and calling on all to go home. A sudden thought struck Bryceson ; he whispered a few words in the ear of Galbraith, who laughed and nodded at his friend as he disappeared round the corner of South Street.

Five minutes later, as a second crowd was forming in a threatening manner before the Town Hall, high above all the storm of cries and shrieks. rang out the sharp clear sound of a bugle. It silenced the mob as if by magic ; again it gave out its warlike message, and that settled the matter. " The soldiers ! the soldiers ! " was the universal cry, and one wild rush was made to the top of the town,

where the leaders of the riot had determined
to face any troops which might be sent. For
an hour they stood on their guard, shouting
defiance, but doing no more mischief. It
was one o'clock in the morning, and all were
pretty well worn out, when the first troops
arrived in answer to the repeated appeals of
the Mayor ; without in the least exaggerating
the danger, he had made such alarming repre-
sentations that two companies of the Guards
had been hastily dispatched by a special train.
They marched into the town, and the riot
was at an end. In every direction those concerned in the work of destruction and plunder
scattered ; a strong force of county police
followed the soldiery next day, and the magis-
trate sat daily receiving information and
granting warrants for the arrest of ring-
leaders. The townsmen breathed freely once
more.

"By Jove, sir !" said an officer of the
Guards to Bryceson, as he laughed at the bugle
stratagem, and praised Ned's mixed drink, " I
never saw a town in the state this was ; what
a spitfire of a place it must be ; upon my word
it only wanted a little blood in the gutters and
a few broken accoutrements scattered about

here and there, to look like a street on the north side of Sebastopol."

Thus was the Avonham election lost and won, and thus did they fight after it was over. It will be many a day before the memory of that day fades from the minds of Marlshire men, and over many a winter's fire the battle is fought again. Sometimes the speaker waxes indignant as he tells of the damage and plunder done on that wild night ; sometimes he chuckles as he relates how glass flew and woodwork crashed in the houses of t'other side. In some cases there are scars to show in proof of what was done, and here and there a man may be pointed out who suffered imprisonment or fine for his share of the mad work. And for years one man would scowl and frown and mutter oaths under his breath as he passed a certain gate in South Street, where rumour said some of the fighting had taken place. He was a tall, dark man with a coarse and vagabondish set of features, who, when he came before any magistrates in those parts, gave the name of Thomas Purcell. He had only one arm.

CHAPTER III.

PROFOUNDLY grateful to the head of their
family were Mrs. Bompas and her three
daughters when the news reached them of the
stirring transactions which had been taking
place in Avonham during their absence. The
country journals had been full of praise of
Mr. Bompas and the Mayor, both of whom,
it was stated, had acted most courageously
in the cause of order, and even the London
papers had followed in the same strain, but
with less diffuseness ; the little Marlshire town
had suddenly earned for itself a most unenviable reputation ; really the quietest and most
decorous of places, it had been likened to a
volcano full of smouldering and dangerous
atoms, liable at any moment to burst forth in
desolating riot and lay the country waste.
The young ladies waxed not a little indignant
over this comparison, and lamented the town's
disgrace, whilst they rejoiced in the praise of

their sire. When that worthy—who stuck
valiantly to his post beside his friend the Mayor
till all the results of the row were investigated ;
till the prominent rioters had been punished
and the town freed from the military control
which for two or three days was deemed necessary, and indeed until Avonham, but for the
glaziers, was quiet again—when Mr. Bompas
joined his family in London he was received
with open arms, not only as one who had
escaped a great danger, but as one who had
comported himself right valiantly therein. He
found an auditory eager to hear all the news
of the fray, and encouraged, unchecked and
uninterrupted, he poured out his warlike tale.

To do Mr. Bompas justice, he was not given
to boasting of his own exploits ; he really and
truly had amply deserved the encomium which
Bryceson had passed upon him of being a
" brick," and had acted like the stout-hearted
old fellow he was ; but he made no great
account of what he had done, and rather slurred
over those parts of the narrative relating to
his own share in the affray. He was full of compliment towards his friend Sennett, and loud in
praise of his two neighbours ; he described the
repulse of the first attack on the " Coombes "

in glowing terms, and praised the coolness and courage of the young men to the skies ; and when he mentioned with the awe which the recollection of the affair still imposed, the Herculean feat which Galbraith had performed with the unfortunate quarryman, his vocabulary of commendatory phrases gave out, and he could only say with uplifted hands, " There, my dears, it was simply marvellous. I could hardly credit my own eyes."

One matter the good old fellow did not mention to his daughters, and that was the ignoble part played in the disturbance by Adolphus Carter. He had been sorely exercised in mind about that unfortunate youth. He had ridden over, in company with his crony Millard (for he did not wish to let the Mayor know of the matter whilst he was engaged in his official capacity in punishing other rioters), to the father of the culprit, and the trio had returned and called on Galbraith, who had condoled with the father and promised to take no more notice of the matter, so that Adolphus was again seated in his employer's office, a very sad and subdued young man indeed. Mr. Bompas, considering that sufficient had been done to humble his pupil, did not attempt to lower him still farther in the eyes of his daughters. But, alas ! what human foresight can prevent a woman from imparting her ideas ? Mr. Bompas, who concealed the story from his daughters, unfolded it to his wife, and that good woman and mother hit the scent at once. She poured into the astonished ears of Mr. Bompas her elucidation of the mystery, and he was forced to accept it. Jealousy, and not politics, was at the bottom of the attack on South Street.

"My dear Abel," she said, "of course it was nothing else ; you needn't go fishing for motives when they're on the surface ; he was jealous of those two young men coming to the house, though, to be sure. Mr. Bryceson has dropped in more often than Mr. Galbraith, and thought he could annoy them in that way ; what a mischievous, ill-natured, spiteful little monkey he is."

Ah, luckless Adolphus ! hitherto so eligible. It was an evil chance for you when this stranger came on your happy hunting ground, it was worse when you conceived your scheme of revenge and failed so ignominiously, but it was the worst of all when Mrs. Bompas took up arms against you. Papa may forgive, papa may forget, but with Mamma arrayed against you, farewell to your hopes.

Great was the surprise, and great the indignation among the young ladies next morning, when Mrs. Bompas, at the breakfast table, told the tale of Carter's attack on the "Coombes" and his overthrow. Which predominated it would be difficult to say, probably the surprise. There was a feeling of pity as the father described to his daughters the shock which his conduct had given to his father; there was a comic side to the picture, as he told them of the prisoner sobbing and grovelling on the floor before his stern captors, and a feeling of admiration for the forgiveness and leniency exhibited by Galbraith. When the girls were next together, in the absence of the old folks, they discussed the matter at length and with much spirit. Adelaide was specially warm on the unjustifiable attack on the "Coombes," and declared that she would never speak to Carter again.

" A mean little rascal." she said, stamping her pretty foot and looking the essence of scorn, " what did he mean by it ? Mr. Galbraith had done him no harm, and papa says he doesn't believe he had been in the town all day, so it couldn't have been connected with the election."

"And certainly," said Louisa, "he could have no cause for injuring Mr. Bryceson."

"Of course not," said Adelaide, "gracious only knows what the little monster *did* mean."

"Will papa keep him, do you think?" said Louisa.

"Not if I can persuade him to get rid of him," said Adelaide, "an odious thing. I always thought there was something monkey-ish in the way he pranked himself up, and chattered and skipped about; I didn't give him credit for so much mischief though; I did think he was harmless enough."

"Papa didn't say anything of Walter Rivers or Alfred Shelman in this matter. I wonder why these two heroes didn't distinguish themselves in putting down the riot?" said Louisa.

"I believe it was all the fault of those horrid Yellows," said Adelaide, "and Alfred Shelman didn't *want* to interfere." She slightly flushed as she mentioned the name.

"And what about Walter Rivers, dear?" said Lucy, demurely.

Adelaide flushed again. "Papa didn't say

that either of them was in the riot. He certainly said, though, that the Yellows began it—why should the Blues have rioted ? They hadn't lost the election—Mr. Rivers might have tried to stop the disturbance but——"

" My dear," said Lucy, composedly, " Walter Rivers is not at all adapted for hurling people over the moon, and I should think was extremely averse to be made a missile of. I can't quite imagine him interfering in a row ; no, I expect the pair of them stayed at home like good little men and took care of their uncles, leaving our interesting neighbours to do the fighting. Everyone to his trade."

" I'm very glad at any rate that we were out of it," said Louisa. " It was an excellent idea of papa to bring us up here. I should like to take a peep at the place, though, and see the damage done."

" Yes," said Lucy, " and we missed the officers too—not that it matters to you two spoons, but there might have been a chance for me."

" What do you mean by spoons ? "

" Whom are you calling spoons, Lucy ? "

This from both the elder sisters. Not with

any irritation—oh, dear, no—only the pretence
of it.   Lucy was "chaffing," but Lucy was
the privileged satirist of the family, and it is
not always unpleasant to be twitted in love
matters.

"Oh, my dears," said Lucy, "do you think
your little sister hasn't eyes ?   Mr. Galbraith
meets you, Addie, going to Beytesbury and
convoys you home, to use dear papa's phrase
—well—what's the consequence ever since ?
Just let anyone mention the man's name suddenly when you're sitting thinking—it's like
dropping a half-crown in a beggar's hand—
only the beggar doesn't blush and *does* thank
you——"

"Lucy, you're a goose."

"And then there's Lou."

"Now you let me alone, Miss Lucy."

"Just ask someone to watch your face and
report on it the next time that Mr. Bryceson
walks in—to see mamma, of course—to get
something for his lungs—his lungs, indeed.
Louisa, my dear child, you're a much better
doctor than mamma is.   *You* know his lungs
are all right, don't you ?   Of course you do !
It's the heart that's affected, and you're looking
after it very skilfully, my love."

"Addie, what shall we do with this girl? she's incorrigible."

"I don't know. Look at her now, Lou. Lucy, who ever taught you to wink? You'd better not practise in London."

Miss Lucy slowly opened the eye which she had really closed in a very knowing manner at the end of her speech, and nodded her head very slowly and sagely two or three times, then she rose and clasping Adelaide round the waist gave her a sisterly kiss, next turned to Louisa and did the same for her, all without speaking a word.

The two elder sisters turned very red, and —kissed each other. The sweet little secret was out; the thin veil was drawn aside by the hand of this laughing sister. That golden hour of life was begun which follows the first confession of love.

Then came papa, eager for sight-seeing, and with many plans for their holiday together. Papa was in the best of humours. Papa was not at all afraid of the Regent Street shops. Papa was eager to please his pretty daughters, and ready to pull his purse-strings wide. If the sisters did not describe their parent by the epithet applied to him by the absent Bryceson, yet surely they used the nearest feminine equivalent when they were surveying his purchases at the end of his first day in town. Nor was he content to visit shops alone. It was only necessary to mention a place of amusement or exhibition, and the cheery old fellow trotted off to secure the best places and the cosiest conveyances to and from the show.

" My dear," he said to his wife, as they sat in the back of the box at the opera, and watched their three girls entranced by the music and spectacle, " we do not visit the great metropolis every day, and it shall not be my fault if the girls, aye, and you, my dear, do not thoroughly enjoy yourselves. It is many years ago since we first beheld these scenes together."

" More than I care to remember always, Abel."

" Well, my dear, they have been very happy ones for me. If our girls only get on as well as we have, they will have but little to complain of. At present they are with us, and we must make the most of them. We must not look forward to many more years of their society."

" I suppose not, Abel, if everyone is going

to admire them as much at home as abroad. If I've seen one opera glass pointed this way I've seen fifty."

"My dear," said Mr. Bompas, gallantly, " I noticed the same thing with their mother more than five-and-twenty years ago, in this identical place."

Mrs. Bompas laughed, but appeared pleased with her faithful spouse. The girls, engrossed in the opera, had not caught their parents' conversation, and she felt safe in proceeding.

"Abel," she said, "do you know I fancy Adelaide seems a good deal taken up with young Mr. Galbraith."

"Well, my dear, I have observed symptoms of embarrassment when the gentleman's name has been mentioned, which would seem to confirm your idea."

"Well, Abel, what do you think of it ? "

"Upon my word, my dear, I have not given the matter attention enough to say what I really *do* think of it."

"I suppose Mr. Galbraith is well off ? "

"That I suppose, but it is only a—ah— surmise. He is purchasing property, which —ah—looks like it, and he is also—a—paying for it, which again seems to hint at the possession of money. Of course, if such a matter as you seem to contemplate were to be brought before me, why then—of course—as a father, it would be my duty to—ah—de-li-cate-ly investigate Mr. Galbraith's position, but at present, my dear, of course I can only guess at his means from his manner of living, which appears comfortable, and even, in some respects, lux-u-ri-ous."

The thoughts of the delicious draughts which Edward's deft hands had compounded rose up before him and compelled the last epithet. He seemed to scent the fragrant drink, and hear once more the ice tinkle on his goblet brim.

" Well, Abel," pursued the faithful mother, " our girls are very good girls, and ought to marry well, and they're getting very much admired here in London. Young Mr. Goldings was most attentive to Adelaide the other evening, and we go there to-morrow, you know. The dear girl won't want for strings to her bow, I can see. I'm very glad we've had this little trip. It'll show them a little of the world, and let them know there are other places besides Avonham, and attractions out-side their own home."

Just then the crash of applause broke in at

the final chorus of the act, and conversation
in the box became general.

Mr. Bompas had, of course, correspondents
in London, and for the most part these were
men whose acquaintance and connection with
him were of many years' standing. Many a
cunning bottle of rare old wine made its appearance in his honour and for his delectation in
Inn chambers, in old-fashioned taverns, and in
the barn-like rooms of Bloomsbury houses, the
cosiest, handsomest and roomiest in London,
but now sadly fallen from their high estate, and
given up to lodgers, mysterious agencies and
money-lending offices dignified with the titles
of banks, and having an evil savour attached
to most of their names. In those old houses
twenty years ago were to be found dinners and
cellars of irreproachable excellence, and hosts
and diners hard to be equalled in these days
of barrack hotels on the one hand and tardily
repentant abstinence on the other. And the
ladies were as hospitable as the men, as Mrs.
Bompas well knew, and as her daughters were
to experience now ; and heartiest of the hearty
was the welcome extended to Mr. and Mrs.
Bompas and his family by old Mr. Goldings,
.the head of the firm of family solicitors,

Goldings and West, of Lincoln's Inn Fields, who inhabited a mansion in Russell Square. A dinner was, of course, the mode which the solicitor adopted whereby to entertain his friends ; and his womenfolk talked him over into giving a dance afterwards, and to both of these forms of entertainment our Avonham friends were bidden. Two of the daughters of the host were school-fellows of the girls, and five merrier, brighter lassies could nowhere be found.

At dinner-time Adelaide went down with young Goldings, a West - Central Adonis, marked as highly eligible by many a fond mother. This young man was, as Mrs. Bompas observed, very much smitten by the charms of his pretty neighbour, to whom he paid great attention. Adelaide remembered him as a gawky boy of fifteen, home from Charterhouse for his holidays ; he was now a rather good-looking young fellow of twenty-six, the junior partner of the firm, and with very pretty tea-table manners, which became him extremely well. Louisa fell to the lot of his brother, an Oxonian, of mild countenance and gentlemanly manners, who was to all outward appearances likely to develop into a model curate of the non-muscular Christian school, and who consequently cherished in his heart Republican and free-thinking principles and opinions that would have made Thelwall shudder ; these were not produced at table, however. A father who is a family solicitor is touchy on the doctrine of equality, and Republicans are mild in the presence of a tureen.

Lucy's cavalier was the cheeriest of white-haired old bachelors, who apologised for the temporary absence of a favourite nephew, who would, he said, join the party after dinner, but who kept Miss Lucy quite as lively as her sisters seemed with their neighbours. The dinner was of the florid English order, the company the reverse of dull, the host seemed really glad to see his friends, and took wine with his guests in the cheery old-fashioned manner of bygone days that ought not, I think, to have gone with them. Perhaps it survives somewhere, but it is drifting away on that sea of innovation which has washed away the country dance and the punch bowl—more's the pity. But here, in those days, the custom flourished, and no point of its jovial solemnity was omitted. The challenge, the stereotyped acceptance, the " taking in," the beaming smile contemporaneous with the courtly bow over

the brimming glasses, and the simultaneous
draughts, all was carried out that properly
appertained to the good old rite. Mr. Markham, Lucy's partner, was especially selected as
a mark for individual challenges and he never
failed to respond. He was a source of great
amusement to Lucy, who described him afterwards as the dearest old beau she had ever
met ; Mr. Trumphy was nothing to him.

"How long do you stay in London, Miss
Lucy ? " said he ; " I'm not going to call you
Miss Bompas, for two reasons : first of all,
you're not Miss Bompas yet, and next the
name isn't pretty enough for you."

" Thank you for the compliment, Mr. Markham. We shall stop, I hope, for another three
weeks ; this is my first visit to London since
I was at school here."

" Well, you must come out and see my place
at Hampstead ; I shall get your father to bring
you."

" I'm sure papa will be most happy."

" Goldings was telling me about his pluck
at that dreadful riotous place of yours. I
wonder you're not afraid to live there."

" Indeed, it's the quietest place in the world,"
said Lucy, standing up bravely for her native

town ; " I can't make out how it happened ;
we've never had an election there, that I can
remember, and I don't believe it was our
townspeople who made the riot at all."

" Quite right to stick up for your own town,
Miss Lucy ; I've a nephew who has been there
once, and he described it as a very quiet
place."

" It's a very nice place."

" Many young gentlemen there ? "

" Oh ! I don't know ; about the average
number I believe.   There is an average of male
population in the country, isn't there ? I mean
so many males to every female—two and a half
or something of that sort."

Mr. Markham laughed.

" Oh, there is, I assure you ; I learned
something about it at school ; it's a horrid
thing for the men, you know ; they can't all
get married, of course."

" Some of them don't want to, Miss. I've
kept away from it myself, and made room for
someone else, you see."

" Haven't you ever been married, Mr. Markham ? I should have thought you had been,
you seem so nice."

" My turn to thank you for a compliment,

now ; but I think you've got your statistics wrong somehow."

" How ? "

" Why, if I don't mistake, there are more women than men in this country."

" Good gracious, that's worse ; why there isn't a man apiece for all of us ; *we* can't all get married then ? "

" Well, there are old maids as well as old bachelors, you know."

" Yes, but if there aren't any more of one than the other, that makes no difference to the rest, you know."

" Some men marry twice."

" So do some women—we're no better off even then."

" Well, Miss Lucy, I venture to prophesy that you needn't trouble about the scarcity of husbands. Even if there aren't enough to go round for everybody, there'll be someone coming for you, I'm certain. Now, while you're thinking over the one that's coming——"

" There isn't one."

" How do you know ? "

" Well—how you tease—I mean I don't know him, and he hasn't begun to come yet "—and Lucy looked the old gentleman

saucily in the face, and laughed merrily at
him.

"Ah! he'll come some day, perhaps to-
night, who knows? I'm going to ask your
father to take wine with me."

Mr. Markham caught the eye of Mr. Bompas without much difficulty, and the two
handsome old fogies hob-nobbed with a courtly
grace that would put to the blush scores of
the youth of to-day—if youth blush nowadays, which is doubtful.

When the ladies retired, and the gentlemen
closed up to their host's end of the table, Mr.
Bompas found himself next to Mr. Markham,
who complimented him first upon his daughters, and secondly upon his conduct at Avonham. Before they joined the party upstairs,
which was now numerous and ready for the
dance, Mr. Bompas had settled a visit to
Hampstead, and appointed a day for that
purpose.

On reaching the drawing-room, Mr. Markham made his way to Lucy, and laughingly
asked her to pilot him through a quadrille.

"That is my only dance except 'Sir
Roger,'" said he, "but I never like to admit
that my dancing days are quite over."

The first quadrille is a stately and solemn affair which a Bench of Bishops might dance with their Diocesan Secretaries' Aunts, and Mr. Markham went through it as a matter not to be irreverently handled ; at the conclusion of it he gallantly escorted Lucy to a seat, and thanked her for the dance. At that moment a good-looking young fellow, who had just been shaking hands with Mrs. Goldings, came up, and, addressing the old gentleman as " uncle," grasped his hand and shook it heartily.

" Ah, Fred. my boy, only just arrived ? " said the old gentleman. " Quite well ? That's right. Here, sir, let me introduce you to my first partner. Miss Lucy Bompas, this is my nephew, Mr. Frederick Markham. Now, my dear, I can leave you in the hands of a partner who can dance ; take care of Miss Bompas, Fred, and find her plenty of partners."

Lucy and the young fellow were soon whirling round the room, and much as she had liked the uncle, it must be owned that her new partner was more to her liking, so far as dancing went. He put his name down three times on her card, introduced her to fresh partners, danced with her sisters and the daughters of the house, but always returned to her as often as he got a chance.

"What capital dancers all you sisters are," said he, when, having manœuvred them all to the same seat and got ices for them, he lounged by them, much envied by the rest of the young men in the room.

"It must come by nature, then," said Louisa, "for we are terribly short of practice."

"Well, I must ask you to spare me another dance apiece after supper. Pray, are your cards all full?"

"You can have a polka, Mr. Markham," said Adelaide. "I have one here—number 16."

"Many thanks. Miss Louisa Bompas, have you anything to bestow in charity?"

"A schottische. Is that good enough for you?"

"Beggars mustn't be choosers. Number 18, isn't it? Please give me your card. Thank you very much. Miss Lucy Bompas, my uncle told me to take care of you, please give me the supper dance. I will forage for you like a Cossack."

"With pleasure, Mr. Markham. What are you doing with my card? You have put down another after supper."

" I asked for one after supper. Here comes someone to take you away. Don't forget the dance before supper."

"Lucy, my dear," said Adelaide, " how many dances have you given that young man to-night? Six, I believe. Lou, I think the next time this young woman ventures to read her sisters lessons about blushing we must ask to look at her programme."

Presently the supper dance arrived, and, that over, supper itself, to which Lucy and her partner went down in high spirits. Fred was as good as his word, and provided most skilfully for Lucy's wants. When at last he had leisure for conversation he said :

" You are only on a visit to London then, Miss Bompas ? "

" That is all. We live a good way down in the country in Marlshire."

" Marlshire ? Oh, indeed. I was down there for a day not long ago, at Avonham."

" Oh, yes, I remember your uncle told me you were. Well, Avonham is where we live."

" Is it, indeed ; how curious ! Why, one of my dearest friends lives there."

" Who is that ? "

" Harry Galbraith. Do you know him ? "

" Oh, yes, he's a neighbour of ours—and do you really know him, and is he a great friend of yours ? How singular. Do you know the whole town is just dying to know all about him. We used to call him the hermit, and the recluse, and all sorts of names until we knew him and his friend Mr. Bryceson."

" Walter Bryceson is another of my friends."

" Fancy that now."

" And there aren't two finer or better fellows in the world. We were together for many years in America. It was to visit Harry that I went to Avonham. We all dined at the hotel there, and a capital time we had."

" I remember the time you came. Everyone wondered who you all were, and where you all came from ; that is," she added, " all the gossips of the town, at any rate. Papa knows Mr. Galbraith very well. He has done business with him : sold him a house and some land for a lady whose affairs papa manages. Papa says Mr. Galbraith and Mr. Bryceson behaved splendidly the other day in a riot at Avonham. Do you know Mr. Galbraith threw a man right over some people's heads ? He must be very strong."

" He's the strongest man I ever met in my

life, and as brave as a lion. It was not the
first row Harry and Walter have been shoulder
to shoulder in. We've seen some queer things
together, Miss Lucy. Do you know I'm so
glad you live at Avonham. I shall have a
chance of seeing you again."

"We shall be very glad, I'm sure," said
Lucy, casting down her eyes.

"I shall make great use of Harry now,"
said Markham, laughing, "now I've a real
excuse for running down." He lowered his
voice and, bending forward, added, "I can kill
two birds with one stone."

The rest of the night was very sweet to
Lucy. Her programme was, as Louisa told
her afterwards, "a terrible tell-tale;" and she
unblushingly sat out a dance with Fred in
the conservatory whilst the would-be partner
whose name figured on the programme was
wildly hunting for her. Old Mr. Markham,
to whom she gave "Sir Roger," was very
funny over her system of averages and her
statistics; her sisters very facetious in the
carriage going home; that last hand pressure
was indeed sentimental, Adelaide declared;
and even mamma had her little joke. But
the two elder sisters were vastly surprised

when Lucy told them of the old friendship
existing between young Markham and their
two Avonham neighbours. In due time, next
day, arrived Mr. Markham and his nephew—

> "The ball's fair partner to behold,
>   And humbly hope she caught no cold,"

as the old gentleman quoted. The two old
fellows made friends very rapidly, and the
young people were very merry. With a mischievous hint or two Lucy contrived to give
Fred some inkling of the impression his two
friends had made on the hearts of her sisters,
and he discoursed in glowing terms of both of
them. He gave some bright sketches of their
life abroad, and from him the Bompas family
learned many things of the two strangers who
had pitched their tents in Avonham. Mrs.
Bompas was gratified to learn that both Galbraith and Bryceson were wealthy ; not really
mercenary or worldly, she was yet put greatly
at her ease by learning that in addition to the
fortune made in California, each had inherited
family property ; and Fred spoke so eloquently
of the bravery, modesty and large-heartedness
of Galbraith and of the unfailing good humour
and sterling good qualities of Bryceson, that

Adelaide and Louisa were delighted. When the two took their leave of the country family, and the girls were again alone, Louisa said :

" Lucy, your admirer is very nice ; he's a clever man, I'm sure, and I heard his uncle tell papa that he was the best of good fellows to his old father and to him, and he talks wonderfully well—doesn't he, Addie ? "

" Capitally," said Adelaide. " I like him very much."

" Well, his subject was interesting to you two turtle-doves," said Lucy.

" Wait till he talks about you, my dear," said Adelaide, " you'll be more interested then. How curious it all seems. Whatever is going to happen to us three girls ? At present we seem like one joint stock company falling in love with another one."

CHAPTER IV.

A MEETING, A TALK AND A LETTER.

"What a one-horse place this is, Harry," said Bryceson one morning at the breakfast table, as he laid down a letter which Edward had just brought him; "my man in town declares he sent off the guns four days ago, and they must be at Avonham Road. Now I've told that carrier to enquire always for anything for us, and I'll go bail he's never put himself out of the way to do it. What a place of this size wants to be five miles off a railway station for is more than I can make out."

"Well, let us ride over this morning and see about them," answered Galbraith. "Ned was at me this morning about some wine that ought to have turned up on Saturday when he was over there; we may as well go in that direction as another."

"Very well."

"I'm very anxious, too, to hear from the Squire; we must be getting a letter in a few days ; and there's another thing—I've a letter here from Fred Markham."

" Fred ! how's Fred ?"

" Oh, all right, he has met the Bompas people in town and owns to being very much taken with one of 'em."

" Which one ?" said Bryceson very quickly.

" With the youngest," said Galbraith, laughing.

" Oh ! Lucy ; h'm, well, I'm very glad of it ; they're cut out for one another, those two."

Galbraith laughed again : " You're quite brotherly, old fellow ; there was a real family air about that remark."

" Pass me a weed, you old humbug, and look at home. By the way, where did Fred meet them first ?"

" At the house of Goldings—coincidence number two. If we don't hear from Squire this mail I vote for a run to town ; Fred will be glad to see us and we shall be none the worse for a night or two together."

" Seconded and carried."

" Well, let's have the horses and go off to Avonham Road. I want to go over to the builder's in High Street about the loose boxes, and he is sure to be half-an-hour before he understands what I want."

"Let Ned bring them round to the ' Bear.' "

"That house will close and Pinniffer will hang himself when you leave Avonham."

"Suppose I stop here, then, and avoid a catastrophe."

"Let us see how things turn out, old boy ; it's kind enough of you, goodness knows, to be here with me now."

"I don't see it ; I'm in deuced snug quarters ; a good deal cosier than my barrack of a place in Essex. But just fancy old Fred running across the Bompas girls."

"The world's very small," said Galbraith sententiously ; "come along to my bricks-and-mortar friend. Ned, bring the horses to the ' Bear ' in half-an-hour."

"Do you know anything of that man ? " said Bryceson as they passed the Bank and saw Shelman standing at the door in conversation with a customer.

"Not any more than I want to," said Galbraith ; "he's an ill-conditioned, surly fellow at the best. I had some communication with him when I first came here—he wanted the ' Coombes,' you know."

" Yes, you told me."

" Well, he wanted that chestnut horse, and
didn't get it, and the other day he wanted
that land and didn't get that either, and to
tell you the truth, Walter, I've been putting
two and two together, and I fancy I can trace
the attack on the house the other night to
him."

" Hallo ! "

" I only want to get that ex-prisoner of
ours in a corner one day and I shall get it out
of him, I have no doubt."

" And then ? "

" And then I'll give the young gentleman
about as good a cow-hiding as he deserves.
I'll make sure first though. He's a nasty-
tempered brute, I hear, and very fond of
threatening people who offend him ; Ned has
heard some of his remarks about me at second-
hand in this tattling, gossiping, mischief-
making hole, and loves the fellow about as
much as I do. Have you run across him
much ? "

" Once or twice—I'm not smitten with him
myself. If you're away at any time, and the
cow-hiding seems needful, I shan't have any
compunction in acting as your deputy."

" Thank you, old boy ; it couldn't be left in
better hands. Come in with me now, and help
me make this architectural genius understand
what a loose box is. I believe he has a sort of
idea that it has hinges and a lid to it."

The local builder, however, was more en-
lightened as to the edifice he was expected
to erect, and the friends, having interviewed
Mr. Pinniffer and tasted his cherry brandy,
mounted and rode off towards Avonham Road
Station. Neither the horses nor the riders at
the " Coombes " were in the habit of being
passed on the road, and all vehicles and horsemen going in the same direction were overtaken
and left behind as a general rule. About mid-
way between the town and the station, the
carriage of Mrs. Stanhope was seen ahead. It
was rapidly overhauled, and as Bryceson
dashed past in front of his friend, he saluted
the gentleman seated by the side of the widow.
The two friends had dismounted and handed
their steeds to a brace of rustics who were
hovering round the station on the look-out for
a job, when the equipage they had passed drove
up, and Mr. Walter Rivers alighting, gave his
arm, in turn, to Mrs. Stanhope and to his
uncle. As the two latter went into the station

Walter Rivers came up to Bryceson and held out his hand.

"How do you do, Mr. Bryceson? I have been anxious to see you. I didn't notice who you were just now, until you had passed and my uncle told me."

"Let me introduce my friend and host, Mr. Galbraith," said Bryceson.

The two young men bowed.

"Mr. Galbraith, the town has to thank you greatly for your exertions in the cause of order the other night. I'm sorry to hear that your property suffered. Will you come inside and let me introduce you to my uncle, who is most anxious to know you?"

Galbraith and Bryceson followed Rivers into the waiting-room, where Sir Headingly and Mrs. Stanhope were standing. Sir Headingly shook hands with Bryceson, and was introduced to Galbraith, whom he greeted cordially. Rivers then approached Mrs. Stanhope and presented the two friends to her.

"Mr. Galbraith," said she, as she returned that gentleman's bow, "it seems remarkably strange that we have never met though such important transactions have taken place between us. It has really been through the

fact of all my business being undertaken for
me.   I am very pleased to meet you now,
though ; you and your friend are quite the
heroes of the place.   Did they damage your
house much ? ''

"No, madam," said he.

"I hear that you requited your injuries on
some of your opponents, Mr. Galbraith," said
she, smiling.

"Oh, yes, madam, I generally manage to
pay any little debt of that description in full."

"Are you going to town by any chance,
gentlemen ? " said Sir Headingly.

"No," answered Bryceson, "we are only
looking after some things which we have
ordered from London ; it is very awkward
having no station at Avonham itself."

"I trust that that will be speedily remedied,"
said Sir Headingly, rather stiffly (the con-
founded railway had been dinned into his ears
a little too frequently lately).

"I see you have your horses, or I would
place my carriage at your disposal," said Mrs.
Stanhope graciously, as her footman approached
Sir Headingly and handed him the tickets ;
" good day, gentlemen."

The two friends bowed to the stately lady

as she moved off on the arm of Sir Headingly, who shook hands with them, as also did Rivers ; the party then crossed the line by the bridge and awaited the up train.

Bryceson invaded the booking office and began stirring up the slow-going porter-clerk, who presided lumpily over the parcel department ; having succeeded in identifying the gun cases and wine cases, which the sleepy old local carrier had omitted to bring over to the " Coombes," and having rapidly given the officials at the station his opinions on their method of conducting business, he rejoined his friend just as the up train containing the party moved off.

" I wonder what that dear creature would say and do if she had the slightest idea of who and what I am, Walter ? " said Galbraith, when they had ridden two or three hundred yards from the station on their homeward way.

" I can't say, old fellow ; of course there will be a tremendous explosion when the exposure takes place."

" I don't know. I think, though, that matters are likely to be precipitated."

" How ? "

" Why, I rather fancy—I've only taken the

idea into my head just now—that the amiable lady intends to marry again."

" The deuce you do !   Whom ? "

" That young spark to whom you introduced me just now."

" What makes you think that, Harry ? " said Bryceson, slightly checking his horse in his surprise, and looking extremely astonished at hearing his friend's opinion.

" Frankly, old fellow, I can hardly tell you. One of those impressions of mine, I think, that used so often to come right over yonder ; though, of course, there is more foundation for this idea than there was for a good many of them.   The young fellow is a very eligible match ; so is t'other party, if it weren't for some circumstances which you and I know, and there was a fatherly air towards the pair of them about that baronet friend of yours to-day which I didn't like at all."

" What would you do, Harry, if you knew——"

" That they were going to be married— humph ! I was just asking myself that ques- tion, and be hanged if I shan't find some diffi- culty in fishing up a satisfactory answer to it.   I'm in a quandary over it, I can tell you."

" As how ? "

" This way.   Squire says that he is certain Reginald will recover—recover entirely ; and that time and his treatment have tended to work a complete cure.   Well, now who's to know what his mind will be towards this woman, whom I believe, and you believe—and with precious good reason—to be the very woman who was his wife and drove him mad. When I followed her trail (and I never worked harder at anything) I was animated by a feeling that I was going to get level with a woman who had practically killed Reginald, and I felt like the Avenger of Blood.   When I had tracked her down to this quiet little English town, where no one would have dreamed of finding her unless they had traced her step by step as I did, I took the very best means of concealing from her any suspicion, any thought, of who I might be, by acting in what, when the matter is all over, people will say was the most idiotic and short-sighted manner possible."

" That was——? "

" Buying property of her—and just see how curiously things turn out.   Why, since we know that Reginald is alive, if things are as we suspect, I have no title to the very house which I bought and paid for, to the mere tables at which we eat, or the beds we lie upon. If I had set myself to do this thing deliberately as part of my plan, I could not have succeeded better. When I found out that the Squire and Tom Reynolds and Ralph Derring were in England, and I had arranged with you and Fred to come and meet them at Avonham— you remember the letter—I went into your favourite shanty here (the ' Bear ') to order a dinner."

" Dev'lish good dinner, too, old Pinniffer gave us. Well ? "

" Well, whilst I was there, that little prying, sharp-eyed fellow came in — Rapsey — and began talking scandal. The point turned upon your friend Rivers and that amiable youth Shelman, whom everybody seems to be afraid of except old Bompas, who really is a good old fellow and, I should say, came of a good old stock."

" Well, he's got a very good young stock come of *him*, anyway."

" Very true, Walter. However, to go on with my yarn ; this little man dropped some hints about some rivalry existing between these

two young men, apart from politics; that is
to say, that there was a woman in the case;
the little chatterbox was pulled up very
sharply by some of the people there, and
particularly by Mrs. Pinniffer, for mentioning names or even hinting at them. I took
an opportunity of having a chat with Mrs.
Pinniffer over it afterwards, and got at the
facts. It had been supposed, she said, that
Shelman and Mrs. Stanhope would have been
married, but whether she rejected him or he
didn't feel confident enough to propose she
couldn't say. About Rivers she had, or pro-
fessed to have, no idea in that connection;
that, she said, was some nonsense of Rapsey's
imagination, though she admitted that the
little beggar did at times get hold of some
extraordinary information. It was the meeting to-day that put it into my head, and of
course I may be wrong."

" But if right ? "

" Then comes in my difficulty "—his brow
darkened a moment, and he bit his lip before
going on. " If my original intention had been
carried out in its entirety, the revenge I would
have taken on that woman would not have
been checked by a single scruple. I would

have set my heart as a flint, and have served her as she served him, remorselessly and without pity ; and to let her marry again, to let her enjoy her fancied triumph for a brief—a very brief—time, and then to dash away from her her new happiness would have been a splendid return for her crime. I would, too, have been as pitiless towards the object of her love as towards her, and I would have flung justice to the winds. When a man doesn't study mercy he's bound to lose his grip of justice, I think. He should have been involved in her fall, and should have shared her fate."

They rode on in silence for some time. Bryceson had seen the grief of his friend for his brother many times, and knew how his bright manner and natural cheeriness was often overclouded by this shadow of his life, and what a different being he was under its gloomy influence. Of the band of friends who had clung so faithfully together in many weary wanderings, and many wild scenes, no one had taken more hold of the affection and respect of them all than he. Strong amongst giants, brave amongst heroes, quick and fertile of resource among men of impulse who carried

every day their lives in their hands, Henry
Galbraith had shown himself one of those born
pioneers and leaders of men found in every
new colony, ruling unconsciously by force of
example, and looked up to in crisis and
danger, as men of old looked to their gods for
instant and personal aid. But ever and again
would return the memory of the brother he
had lost, and a paroxysm of rage or a tempest
of grief would sweep across his mind and
change his nature for a while, so that he
would leave friends and companions for a day
together, and, withdrawing himself from the
very sight and sounds of men, meditate his
wrong and brood over revenge, alone and
unfit for companionship. Since the news of
his brother being alive, and the hopeful view
taken of his condition by their old leader, these
moods had disappeared, and he was now looking forward to their meeting with a keen joy
scarcely concealed under the calm and imper-
turbable manner of his communication with
the outward world. Sometimes, however, he
would return to something of his old abstraction, though it lasted but for a short while,
and at such times his faithful friend, who
well knew its cause, was silent until the fit

had passed off, as he was now for some minutes, during which they covered a mile of ground.

"Those, you see, Walter," he went on presently, " were the feelings with which I came here, but since we had that meeting, and the Squire told us how he had found Reginald, and how the dear old chap had tended him and got him better, all the while afraid to let me know in case his care was unavailing, somehow I feel different about it. I don't feel any different towards her," he said, raising his voice and clenching his right hand as if he caught something hostile and gripped it hard ; " she deserves all the punishment she could ever have had at my hands, and, by Jove ! if it rests with me to administer it, it will be short and sharp ; but it won't entirely if Reginald has really recovered ; and I've another thing to say about it—I've no wish to drag anyone else in it who isn't in already. No, if I were to hear for certain that she were going to marry any decent fellow, I would bring matters to a head at once. It would be an instalment of punishment for her, and, as you said just after we left her, there will be a tremendous explosion when the exposure *does* take place. Well, let it take place without hurting anyone but her. I'll take care it reaches her, at any rate."

" Harry," said Bryceson, after a minute's silence, " do you know, there's one thing that just flashed across my mind when you mentioned the fact of your bad title to the house you have bought."

" What was that, Walter ? "

" Of course the title would be bad on account of her not being legally married to Stanhope."

" Of course ; her husband was living at the time."

" Harry, suppose that when she ran away from Reginald with that scamp—suppose, I say, that she got a divorce over in the States ? "

Galbraith checked his horse sharply, and pulled up, as though he had seen a dead body in the road. Walter stopped as well, and for a minute or two the two men looked at each other, Bryceson with a half-puzzled expression as though uncertain how his companion would take the query, Galbraith with a wide stare of blank astonishment. Then Galbraith spoke slowly, and as if with difficulty :

" By heavens, Walter ! I have never thought of that."

"It is possible, though," said Walter, walking his horse on.

"Yes," said Galbraith, following his example, and ranging up to his side, "possible enough, and easily enough to be managed, as we know, but is it probable?"

"Why not?"

"Well, so far as Tom Reynolds always said, the chase was hot-foot after them. Reginald was supposed to have been killed by that scoundrel, and they left the States for Havannah from New Orleans. Now when the first of the guilty pair met his deserts, they were not together. She had been as fickle to the scoundrel her lover as she had been to the good fellow her husband. She would only get a divorce for the sake of marrying the Frenchman, and I know from the inquiries which I made just before his death, that they were never married."

"What you say is true, but she may have got a divorce for all that. You see she has married again, and she may have taken the precaution to secure her position although she did not marry the man who first ran away with her. Consider, old fellow, she left Reginald in '46; in '49 we went to the Pacific Slope, and stayed there till '56; that's three years ago, and here we are in '59. Now, it's thirteen years ago since it happened. Mrs. Stanhope was married, according to the statement of our two friends, Bompas and Millard, about eight or nine years ago. She was married about four years, and has been a widow for about four years—say nine years for the two states—that leaves four years to account for between her flight and her appearance as a decorous married woman in Avonham. Now, Harry, I know you've taken all the pains possible to track this woman, but, of course, old fellow, you found here and there an interval for which you can't fully account. In one of those intervals she may have gone back to the States and sued out a divorce. By George! it's done there every day."

"Well, the supposition is a staggerer, and when I go over, which I shall do soon whether I hear from the Squire or not, I must try to find out. Of course there are records to be had in every State, though some of them must be very loosely kept and hard to get at. Anyhow, Walter, we don't entirely lose our hold of her. I'll not be baulked of my long-expected reckoning. Her record won't bear repeating at any rate, and, by Jove, the task of proving her divorce shall be on her shoulders, and I'll make this side of the Atlantic warm for her till she does."

They rode on without farther conversation until they reached Avonham, which had re-sumed the quiet and sleepy appearance common to it. There were not a dozen people in the street; a few were listlessly standing at the doors of their shops, as if waiting for a wave of commerce to break on their silent shore. If that wave had come it would have swept them away, their old ideas could never have stemmed it. John Rann, from the steps of the market-place, nodded to Mr. Pollimoy forty yards lower down the street, who was standing at his door watching the two horsemen pass. The worthy host of the " Bear " also lounged in the gateway of his tenement, and from that commanding position raked the town with his glance. Him presently the two nodding friends espied, and with expressive signs one to the other disappeared each for a moment, Rann to lock the inner gate, and Pollimoy to don his hat. Then they sauntered up the street to-gether, like two cows who have for a moment pretermitted the absorbing interest in landscape possessed by their race, and wend slowly side by side, apparently without any common object or interest, towards the drinking place. How often this had been done at nearly the same hour every day by these two would be hard to say. See them as they pass along; Timothy Rapsey comes across the churchyard about this time—there he is; Wolstenholme and Hoppenner Pye leave their yard and should be at the Canal Wharf about the same time that the other three reach the steps of the "Bear." Occasionally a rainy day, or snow lying deep in winter, will throw one of these old fellows back a minute, or goad him into an increase of speed, which lands him at the bar parlour door just that space of time ahead of his cronies; if this should happen he remarks it; explains the reason to his friends; makes an incident of it. Market day upsets these arrangements entirely; market day upsets everything; life on market day is passed under conditions other than normal; market day is a vortex drawing in other than Avonham atoms —you cannot be methodical in a whirlpool. But to-day all are punctual. All shake hands, all wait at the gateway till the party is complete (a rainy day alters this as well), and all

tramp stolidly in and greet Mrs. and Miss
Pinniffer, who are at their posts and waiting.
To them all presently enters Mr. Raraty, whip
in hand, and conversation is general.

They have chatted for half-an-hour, when
the far-seeing and sharp-eyed Timothy gives
notice that Mr. Galbraith's black servant is
coming up the street. Two or three of them
stroll to the large bay window, glass in hand,
and observe his movements. He crosses the
market-place and disappears for a few minutes.
The conversation turns upon his master, or
masters, for he seems to have two ; Mr. Rapsey, still observant of the street, suddenly gives
a sharp " hush," and the negro walks in at the
front door, and puts his head into the room ;
he looks round and catches Mr. Raraty's eye—
that worthy goes out to him and receives his
message.

" Will you take anything this morning, Mr.
Edward ? " says Raraty, as he makes an entry
in his note-book.

Mr. Edward is not proof against the invita-
tion and stays. Mr. Rapsey, desirous of information, and guessing by Mr. Raraty's use
of his pocket-book that some posting business
is on hand, hazards the question :

"Mr. Galbraith going on a visit, Mr. Edward!"

"Yes, sah," replies the negro, shortly.

"London?" Mr. Rapsey ventures mildly, while the others interestedly listen.

"No, sah," replies the negro, "dat place whar dey catch dem bloaters—whar's dat?"

"Yarmouth," says Pollimoy, the traveller.

"Yarmuf, dat's it, shuah 'nuf. Massa he goin' dah for to git some dey bloaters fo' de ribber at de back heah; he fink dey do fus' rate in dat water. Mornin', Massa Ra'ty; mornin', gen'l'men."

That afternoon Galbraith and Bryceson drove in Mr. Raraty's dog-cart to Avonham Road, and Edward brought back the trap alone. After Mr. Rapsey's rebuff of the morning, that sable retainer was not over-burdened with questions, it being felt that there was an elaboration of answer about him, which was apt to make the interrogator look and feel somewhat foolish.

The letter from the Squire had arrived, and Galbraith had started in response to it. Avonham would not see him again for some time.

CHAPTER V.

A TRIPLE ALLIANCE.

"HARRY, did you ever meet a man named Jones ?"

"Yes, three or four ; which one do you mean ?"

"Oh, the man I mean was hanged."

"The deuce he was ! I don't remember him ; what was he hanged for ?"

"For not passing the bottle, old fellow, and it served him right, too."

Galbraith roused himself with a laugh, and passed the wine to his friend Markham, who had "sold" him with this old joke, partly to obtain the desired wine, and partly to rouse him from the profound reverie into which he had fallen.

"I beg your pardon, old fellow. I was dreaming, I think ; Walter's yarn sent me to sleep. Ring the bell, Walter ; buzz that bottle and let us start a fresh one."

The three young men were seated in a

private room of the " Star and Garter ; " the
dinner was over and from the lips of two of
them light, curling, blue wreaths had for the
past half hour ascended in graceful spirals
towards the ceiling, fanning out as they
reached the upper currents of air into slowly
vanishing cloudlets ; only from Galbraith
came neither smoke nor sound ; he sat facing
the window, looking fixedly at that glorious
landscape of leafy sheen and silver stream that
is so familiar, yet so ever new, so hackneyed,
yet so refreshing to the smoke-dried, work-
beaten Londoner ; for a quarter of an hour, at
least, Walter had been chatting with Fred
upon various subjects, without the duologue
being once interrupted by their silent friend,
and, as we have seen, the bottle had been
neglected as well as the conversation ; but he
roused himself now at the cheery summons of
his comrades, and shook off the gloom that had
lately seemed to surround him.

"I'm a pretty host, by Jove ! " he said,
rising after Walter had pulled the bell handle
and the soft-footed waiter had appeared.
" Another bottle of burgundy, waiter. What
a jolly view from this window, boys—I don't
know anything prettier. Yes, I do though,

by Jove! and when old Ganymede comes
we'll drink to their pretty eyes, bless 'em!
Walter, if you weren't beyond blushing years
ago you ought to call some of Fred's colour to
your cheeks. Did you ever see a fellow harder
hit? Well, she is a pretty little lassie—they
all are, in fact, and I expect you've chosen to-
morrow's visit to your uncle's for a declaration
—isn't that so? And Walter is just as bad.
Why don't we ask the old folks down here to
dinner? I'll play propriety and keep them in
tow whilst you inveigle Miss Louisa and Miss
Lucy into snug corners, and learn your fate."

"Listen to him, Fred," said Walter, holding
out his hand towards him; "who would think
that civilisation and Europe could have made
such a hypocrite of our old Downright Dun-
stable? He was just as solemn, I assure you,
the night we sat under the verandah at Avonham and he told me how much he admired
Adelaide, and directly——" here the speaker
paused and laughed.

"Well," said Galbraith, laughing in his turn,
"directly what?"

"Directly you suspect us of——"

"Suspect—oh my!"

"Hold your tongue and don't interrupt,

Harry; directly you get it planted into your old head that Fred and I admire your— your——"

" Future sisters-in-law," said Fred.

" Thank you, Fred—directly you get that in your venerable poll we have to put up with fatherly counsel from a prospective brother. Fred, we'll rebel—we won't stand it."

" Well, here comes the wine," said Harry ; " we won't let this bottle stand at any rate ; shall we drink papa and mamma first, or our fairer Avonham friends ? Pity there isn't another for old Ralph Derring—Tom Reynolds is married and done for, so it's no use wishing for a fifth for him, and the Squire is a confirmed old bachelor. Come, boys—bumpers— to their bright eyes, all of 'em—and now for another cigar. I haven't much more time with you, old fellows."

" Nonsense," said Fred, " you'll be back in a couple of months, and Reginald with you ; don't think any more of your troubles and things will turn out all right yet, I'll warrant."

" Let's hope so," said Walter ; " here's good luck to to-morrow anyhow. How jolly that river looks with the sun on it, and that avenue

of trees with the leaves just turning colour—
Harry, you'll just be in time for the Indian
summer over yonder. We shall think of you
down at Avonham, when we're ordering our
first fires to be lit."

"Well, old man, you won't think of me
more than I shall of you. I shan't get far
enough West for the old places, but I think
there will be something in the very soil that
will remind me of old times."

" Ah ! we had some ups and downs there,"
said Fred.

" Yes, but we had some rare luck too."

" Ah, yes, we stuck to work and the luck
stuck to us," answered Bryceson ; " we deserved
all we got."

" I often wonder how it was we outstripped
every other party wherever we had a claim,"
said Fred. " I suppose it was because we
were always leal to each other and worked
for the common good."

" That's so, and we didn't fool around the
camps after work was done, card-playing and
drinking," said Galbraith.

" Well, they were grand times after all,"
said Walter.

" They were," said Galbraith; " by Jove, it's

the best way for a man to spend his young
manhood ! You've room to breathe, and you
can breathe all you want to. You must be
always on the look-out for the next thing that
turns up, and have your eyes and ears open
and your hand ready all day long ; you're face
to face with Nature in her wildest mood, and
man in his roughest form. There's always
something to conquer every day when you get
up, and you've always done something tangible
when you lie down at night. So much dirt
washed, so much rock holed, so many feet of
sluicing done, so many specimens assayed, so
many little shining lumps put away in the
little leather bag the dear old Squire used
to carry. And then the surroundings—who's
forgotten the smell of the pine woods ; who
doesn't remember the cañon where we struck
our first pocket, and how we used to sit snug
when the pack trains passed, and how we lived
at top and threw everyone off the trail by pre-
tending that fur and bear-meat was our little
enterprise ? Gad ! it's something to look back
upon that struggle with Mother Earth herself
to make her yield up the wealth that she has
been hiding up for so many hundred years.
She'll hide us at last, but we've had our good

turn from her first. They won't come again ;
but they were glorious times. There have
been giants on the earth in our time, boys,
and we've done our share of their work ! "

" Yes," said Fred, " and now we are going
to settle down and live like good boys on the
proceeds of our toils. We're like Jack of the
Beanstalk ; we have ventured into the strong-
hold of the giant, and brought away our
treasure ; now for the ' lived-happy-ever-after '
portion, which always winds up the tale."

There was much more chat of the same
nature between the friends before they returned
to London. Galbraith was to sail that week,
and this was a farewell dinner to his two old
comrades ; it was felt by all that the presence
of a fourth person, unless, indeed, he had been
one of the old band, would have been calculated
to throw a damper over the conversation and
party, and for this once the friends were
alone. The Avonham ladies had been considerably fluttered during the past weeks by
finding that two of their neighbours had
followed them to town. Papa had gone to
call on Mr. Goldings and had found them at
his office—quite by accident of course—and
they were invited to the house of old Mr.

Markham on the same day as that fixed for their own visit there, and it would be hard to say whether pleasure or surprise predominated in the minds of the three sisters when they heard the news. Since then they were constantly meeting. Mrs. Bompas looked fidgettily happy, and the worthy head of the family was evidently burdened with thoughts too deep for colloquial expression ; even the heavy artillery of his grave eloquence failed to carry the wordy missile of explanation along the whole range of cogitation.

It was, however, a very merry party that assembled at Fairlawn on the following day ; needless to say that the ladies looked charming, that old Markham was boisterously hospitable, and that the affair was not suffered to drag for lack of light-heartedness. The day was one of those bright September ones that early autumn brings, as if to show how bright she can be, and that her first resplendent dress becomes her as much as the many-tinted robe she will don when her longer life has brought the shortening days ; and the evening had that calm sweet influence that follows a rosy, flaming September sunset, as the sweet voice of the soprano follows the crashing chorus of

the men. Somehow—insensibly of course—
the couples had paired properly off, the old
folks sat talking by the opened window, the
young ones strolled or sat in the grounds.
Not a very long time passed before Fred and
Lucy began to speak in tones that were lower
and lower, though no one was there to listen,
and the pauses between the words were longer
and longer, and the words sweeter and sweeter,
till presently the dainty waist was encircled,
the dainty fingers pressed, the pouting lips
kissed, and the fair head drawn down till it
rested close to the faithful heart. This wild
bird came to the lure as readily and willingly
as the tamest of barn-door fowls. Then after
a short, delicious silence, there was some
pretty business with a ring, and a morsel—
just a morsel—of golden hair, and Lucy had
found fate and mate at once.

"I wonder," said Fred, after awhile,
"whether any more of this sort of thing is
going on anywhere else in the grounds."

"I think," said Lucy, shyly, as if there
were any doubt about the matter, "I think
Mr. Bryceson and Louisa are in the conservatory ; shall we go and join them ? "

"Not for the world, dearest," answered

Fred ; " I wouldn't interrupt them on any account. I think we can guess what is taking place in there—eh, darling ? "

This is what was taking place :

" Do you believe in the language of flowers, Mr. Bryceson ? "

" Not a bit—do you ? "

" I—I—don't know."

" I think it is great rubbish, don't you ? "

" Well—n-o-o—I can't quite say I think it is rubbish ; it may be—perhaps some people carry it—believe in it, I mean, too much, but it's—oh, really, Mr. Bryceson, it's too pretty an idea to be described as rubbish."

" Well, perhaps it is. Maybe I don't understand it enough, either to appreciate it or to do it justice. But, do you know, I think if I wanted to make love to anyone—I say *if* I wanted to make love to anyone——"

" We-e-ll ? " (a very long word).

" Well, I think I'd have sense enough to get through the business without bothering the gardener."

" I'm afraid you're not fond of flowers."

" Oh, but I am—you should see the magnificent tropical fellows—have you ever seen a magnolia—no ? what a pity ! I don't think

anyone knows what floral beauty really is till
he's seen a magnolia."

" Indeed ? " (Not an overwhelming interest exhibited in magnolias.)

" Oh, yes ; I always went into raptures
over the tropical beauties—I mean of flowers,
of course. Now, Harry would sooner have
an English primrose or a violet than any
exotic."

" Really ? " (with some farther loss of interest). " Mr. Galbraith seems quite an important person with you and Mr. Markham."

" Important ! I should think he was—why,
he's the best and dearest fellow in the world.
Important ! I should just—why, do you know,
Lou—I *beg* your pardon—Miss Louisa "—
(both rather red here)—" neither Fred nor I
would be here to-day if it hadn't been for
him."

" What a dreadful life that must be abroad.
Aren't you very glad it's all over ? "

" Oh, I don't know." (*Oh!*) " It was a
glorious life—Harry was saying so only yesterday at Richmond. We went down to the
' Star and Garter ' yesterday, and had dinner
with Harry."

" On Sunday ?—you abandoned men ! "

"Well, you must eat on Sunday. Didn't you eat yesterday ?"

"Of course I did. We had dinner at home."

"Well, but we haven't any home to go to, you know."

"No home ? "

"In London, at least. Of course, we have homes, all three of us—Fred's in chambers, but they're awfully cosy and comfortable ; my house is in Essex."

"I have heard you say so. You don't seem to care for it much."

"I don't—at least, the house is all right, and is a very pretty old place, but then, you see, I haven't anybody to look after it, except a housekeeper and some old servants of my father. Now, if I were married it would be different, wouldn't it ? "

"I—suppose—it—would."

"Of course it would ; it would alter things entirely. I say, Miss Louisa, talking of being married—"(*coming*)—"talking of being married, does your sister—your eldest sister, I mean—"(*Gracious goodness, whatever is coming?*)—"care at all for Harry, do you think ? " (*Oh!*)

" Really, Mr. Bryceson, I can't say. Suppose you ask Mr. Galbraith to ask her."

" Oh, I expect he's doing that now."

" Do you ? "

" Oh, yes. You see, he went down to the lake with your eldest sister, and Fred went into the shrubbery with your youngest, whilst we—came in here."

The dark curls have touched the golden curls ; the dark eyes are gazing very tenderly at the downcast blue ones ; there is a silence that is too full of sweetness for speech.

" Yes, we came in here to talk of flowers. See, here is a meek little one—it is not very gaudy, not like my glorious magnolia, but it has a lovely scent ; may I give you a piece ? "

The little hand takes it silently, and the blue eyes look up, full of love.

" I said just now the language of flowers was rubbish, didn't I ? Well, this little one has converted me. Do you know what the heliotrope means ? "

" Yes "—(a very tiny yes—only just enough to part the rosy lips).

" It means ' I love you '—take my spray, my darling, and put it near your heart—and

25—2

give me a piece in return—and it will mean
that you love me, dearest, as I love you."

All tenderly the little hand plucks the blos-
som, and her face is hidden for awhile.

Down by the lake Galbraith and Adelaide
strolled and talked in much the same manner
as the other two couples. The heart of the
frank girl went out to meet the great love
of this man, so brave, so strong and so true.
When the tender question had been asked
and answered, when heart had beaten against
heart, and lip pressed lip, then Adelaide had
to begin to bear her burden.

"You know I am going away, dearest,
don't you?"

"Oh, Harry! so soon?"

"My darling, it must be so, and I must tell
you why; come, now, let us try whether you
can keep a secret."

And then he told her all.

Few indeed have been the girls who have
had to share in such a secret or to hear such a
tale. It was the shattering of one of Adelaide's
idols for her to be told that the woman to
whom of all women she had been accustomed
to look up with a reverence, partly natural,

partly the result of the surroundings and
traditions of years, was only on a level with
unhappy women the record of whose sins had
only reached the pure heart of the girl as
the sound of the surge on the beach reaches
the listener on the summit of the towering
cliff. But when the first surprise was past,
it filled the heart of her lover with joy
to see the calm way in which she received
the intelligence. This was a woman of
heart indeed. He well knew the courage
and endurance of these quiet souls ; there
would be no need to fear that she would fail
him in either.

"Keep the secret, my darling, for my sake ;
I do not want my dear girl to be a spy upon
another woman, and I will only ask this. If at
any time Walter Bryceson should, during my
absence, be away from Avonham and should
any rumour of her approaching marriage reach
your ears you must at once let him know ; he
will act if I am away."

"Oh, yes, Harry. I'll send for Mr. Bryceson immediately."

"I do not know whether it will be necessary. My impression is that you are going to
see a great deal more of Master Walter than

you think for. Now, darling, let us join your
father and mother."

" I shall see you before you go ? "

" Every day till I leave London—that is,
if papa will have me."

" Oh, there is no fear of that. He is very
fond of you. Oh, Harry, I am so happy.
But I wish you weren't going away. Oh,
here are Lou and Lucy."

Louisa and Lucy, looking most demure
and unconscious, were standing at the open
window talking to Mr. Markham as uncon-
cernedly as if being engaged were a daily experience. Adelaide joined the group, looking
as demure as either of her sisters. The old
gentleman's eyes twinkled.

" Have you seen your mamma, my dear ? I
fancy she has gone out to look for you. Mr.
Bompas, let us go and find some of these
young men and smoke a cigar with them."

When the old boys had left the room there
was a short silence, during which none of the
sisters ventured to look at one another. At
last Lucy spoke in a solemn tone.

" Sisters," she said in a mock-tragedy tone,
" I have a confession to make."

· " Well, dear," from the two others.

" I confess to—having wasted a great deal of time in church."

" What *are* you talking about, Lucy ? "

" Silence, Addie. Yes, my dears, I used to while away the forty minutes of sermon time by reading the service for the solemnisation of holy matrimony—every Sunday regularly."

" Well, madcap, what then ? "

" Louisa, you are not respectful. I am really the steady one of the family. Well, my dears, I read there—bless you, I know it by heart—that it is not by any to be enterprised, nor taken in hand unadvisedly."

" Whatever is——"

" Come and kiss me, my dears, and then let us go and find mamma."

And, as the sisters embraced, a few tears fell, soon dried, but still they fell. You see marriage is an honourable estate and all that, but it wrenches out some good strong roots at times when it transplants young people.

When Mr. Markham and Mr. Bompas encountered their young friends they found them in a high state of spirits, shaking hands wildly all round, and evidently much excited about something. Said boisterous Walter :

" Boys, this makes me feel good. Oh !

Fred ; oh ! Harry, let's get away somewhere quiet and holloa ' Jake Keyser ' till something breaks ! "

" Here's uncle with Mr. Bompas," said Fred. " Let's go straight to papa and out with it."

" Oh ! my dears," said Mrs. Bompas, coming in to her daughters half-an-hour after, " your papa has told me all about it—I'm so happy, my dearest girls—but *please* tell me once more—or write it down, Addie, to make sure— *who's* going to marry *whom*.   You really must sort yourselves out, my dears, or I shall make all sorts of blunders over it."

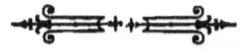

CHAPTER VI.

BEFORE Galbraith took up his abode in Avonham, the inhabitants of that quiet town had
held somewhat singular ideas respecting the
negro race, and, as opinions in Avonham
became, by dint of long holding, elevated and
exalted to the dignity of creeds, it was somewhat of a shock to find that the preconceived
notions and beliefs which had passed current
for so many years were exploded, or, even in
the most conservative of minds, considerably
modified after personal inspection and study
of the specimen of the children of Ham now
residing there.

Mr. Timothy Rapsey was wont to speak of
himself as a student of human nature. With
curiosity the mainspring of his actions, and its
gratification the business of his life, simple and
almost infantile in his manners, he resembled
a child in nothing so much as in the employment of that characteristic of infancy, " taking

a deal of notice." He had the faculty of reception in no ordinary degree ; had he possessed that of retention in the same ratio he would have been a Marlshire Solon ; as it was, although tolerated, and not refused the honour of posing as one of the worthies and authorities of the place, he was forced to admit to himself that he had missed the dignity, the importance, and the gravity which marked the fathers of the town, and distinguished them from the common herd. Yet the town could have better spared a better man than gossiping, inquisitive, prying but amusing Timothy Rapsey, who, just at this period of our tale, was seized with a burning desire to cultivate the acquaintance of Galbraith's negro servant, ostensibly, as he tried to assure himself, with a view of increasing his ethnological knowledge, really, as his mind told him, to gratify his curiosity respecting the inmates of a house which he knew not how to honestly enter and which was now in the charge of Ned. And to know that Galbraith had temporarily vacated his house was not, in Timothy's eyes at least, to know enough, he wished to acquaint himself why he had gone and where he had gone to.

Whilst he was casting about in his mind for

the best means of arriving at this desired end,
and indeed he was not the only Avonhamite
who was curious on the subject, it happened
that the opportunity of gaining a footing with
Ned came about unexpectedly and with
scarcely much of his own seeking. It chanced
one morning, as he was passing the front gate
of the " Coombes," that its janitor, for so he
considered him, was standing at the top of the
steps engaged in paying the carrier, who had
just delivered a parcel. Timothy greeted the
negro with effusion and paused to have a chat
with him, partly to further the great end he
had in view, and partly to find out what had
that morning been left at the house. To his
great gratification Ned entered readily into
conversation, and—the carrier having driven
away—to his still greater glee, after remarking
that the day was hot for the time of year and
that he felt very thirsty, the negro invited
him to enter and refresh himself, promising
him that he would provide him something
grateful and cooling.

When Timothy found himself fairly inside
the mysterious house—for the unknown is
always the mysterious to little minds—he was
fairly beside himself with joy. Everything

was new to him, for he had never visited the
house in Major Currie's time, and whilst Ned
was concerned about the preparation of the
drinks, he peered and pried into every
corner of the room.   Books, pictures, weapons,
strange skins and savage trophies were all
reviewed and commented on in turn, and a
glittering mass of iron pyrites and mica which
Ned produced from a drawer and gravely
assured him was a nugget of pure gold fairly
made him gasp.   Such a cigar as the little
man found between his lips in a few minutes
had never come within his ken, certainly
never found its way to his mouth, and the
first sensation which came over him as he
drew Ned's seductive mixed drink through
the first hollow straw he had used since his
school days, when he had taken half-holiday
draughts from the Avon by means of a similar
apparatus, was akin to his notions of paradise
itself.

When the long tumbler was three parts
empty and the white ash of the incomparable
cigar half an inch long, Mr. Rapsey, according to his usual custom, began to ask questions,
to all of which Ned, placidly smoking and
sipping, affably replied.

He'd been a long time with Mr. Galbraith he said—yes, he had been a slave—no, not kidnapped from Africa—born in America—was born on a Southern plantation—run away? oh, no, never—his ole massa was too kind for that—did Mas'r Galbraiff buy him? oh dear no, Mas'r Galbraiff didn't hold with slavery—no, he'd been a free man many years—been help in a big hotel—Mas'r Galbraiff's brother took a fancy to him and he left to go with him—dead the brother was—oh, yes, he was dead sure 'nuf—yes, he was older than Mas'r Harry — was Mas'r Galbraiff good master? there wasn't such a master in the world. Mas'r Bryceson was a very nice gentleman—yes. the two were great friends—oh, yes, they'd been abroad together—they were both good men—Ned would chop off his right hand for either of them—would Mas'r Rapsey try this other glass? It was a different sort, but just the thing after the other.

Such was the nature of the first portion of the conversation between these new boon companions, and still the white ash grew, and still the drink was good. Mr. Rapsey became more particular and confidential in his enquiries, but still his ebony host answered him freely.

Was Mr. Galbraiff rich ? Oh, yes ; as rich as anyone in Avonham—richer indeed. Didn't know how rich Mrs. Stanhope was. If she were so very rich why did she sell her house and land ? Why not let them ? Had seen Mrs. Stanhope out driving. Mr. Bompas was very nice man—didn't know much about the young ladies' looks—of course he preferred the black girls, or the yellow girls—where was Mr. Galbraiff ? Didn't he tell Mr. Rapsey only a little while ago he was gone to Yarmuf ? Well, he expected he was in London now. What a brave man he was ? Mas'r Harry one of the strongest men anywhere, and brave as a lion—Mas'r Bryceson brave too ; had need to be, both of them, where they'd lived. The rioters hadn't hurt the house much—broken a few windows—he expected some of them had got hurt though—he himself had given one of them a punch in the nose that he wouldn't forget in a hurry—didn't know who set them on to the " Coombes," wished he did know— hoped it was the man whose nose he punched —didn't understand English politics himself— thought England was a very nice place, and liked Avonham very much—yes, Mas'r Galbraiff rode very well, so did Mas'r Bryceson—there were three horses in the stable now ; would Mr. Rapsey like to look at them ? Mr. Pinniffer's man came round twice a day to help—the cook was the groom's wife. Oh, yes, the girl Mr. Rapsey had seen was their niece—yes, she was good girl enough ; she and Mrs. Hackett did all the house work— there were quite enough servants. Mas'r Harry trusted everything to ole Ned, and ole Ned didn't want a whole crowd of womenfolk around ; " don' light dat ar segar 'gain, Mas'r Rapsey, take 'nudder out 'n dat box dar, 'n let me make nudder tum'ler ' Port Royal Sangaree.' "

Mr. Rapsey's eyes twinkled as he lit another famous cigar, after a mild protest, and watched Ned's deft concoction of the delicious draught. When had he had such a morning of delight ? Both his palate and his curiosity gratified, his eyes delighted by the sight of a lump of gold as big as an ostrich egg, his ears regaled with more news than he had been able to extract from anyone for a month, and his thirst slaked with some celestial liquor unknown, he told himself, to even the highest among the great ones of Avonham. Surely a day to be marked with the whitest and largest of all white stones.

And under the combined influence of good spirits, good cigars, and Ned's wonderful mixtures, the heart of the little man opened wide, and with it his mouth. He found as an additional pleasure that the negro made a most excellent listener, that he replied to his local wit with appreciative chuckles and grins, and even with occasional African cachinnations, which not only gratified, but amused him very much. The questions, too, which Ned interpolated now and then proved to the happy little chatterer how much his companion was interested in his conversation, and he laid himself out to repay, with local intelligence and gossip, the sumptuous hospitality he had received at the hands of his host. He gave a description of the principal magnates of the town and their families, considerably heightened and full of local colour. He was not deterred now, in his mention of Mrs. Stanhope, by the restraining presence of Mrs. Pinniffer, and he did not spare his opinion as to the presumed relations between her and the two individuals whom Avonham had set down as her admirers. As a Blue, he hoped Walter Rivers might win the lady, and succeed his uncle in the representation of the borough.

Kept somewhat in a groove by the questions of the negro, he next touched upon the Bompas family, and presented the young ladies with prospective husbands according to his ideas or wishes. It was uncertain which of them Mr. Adolphus Carter was about to be engaged to, he said. He had questioned Mr. Carter on the subject chaffingly only yesterday, and, strange to say, had met with something like a rebuff; the tempers of young men on those points, he said, knowingly, were uncertain, but from the young man's important manner he had reason to believe it would soon be a well-known matter.

Ned grinned hugely at the profound know-ledge of human nature and local matters combined displayed in this remark, and paid Timothy a compliment on his shrewdness, which pleased him highly.

" Really," he thought to himself, " the negro race has been greatly underrated. This man appreciates me a great deal more than half the people in Avonham, who call themselves Christians."

At this juncture Ned changed the subject to the recent election, and asked Timothy whether Carter had had any connection with it.

Mr. Rapsey believed that Adolphus was
very friendly with Alfred Shelman, and that
possibly he might have rendered him some
service in the matter, but that having regard
to his position at Mr. Bompas's, and the fact
that the latter had taken no part in it, he did
not think it probable.

Ned proposed another nice cool Sangaree—
or would Mas'r Rapsey like to taste some real
Bourbon whisky ; there was nothing like it
anywhere else in England, he said.

Mr. Rapsey jovially assented, and added to
his potations a Bourbon straight.

In about half-an-hour Timothy discovered
that he was mixing up the names of a good
many of the people of whom he had been
talking, and he admired more than ever the
great interest evinced in his conversation—
shown chiefly by the gentle way in which he
was every now and again led back into the
right train of thought and coherent speech
by the listener—he became confidential about
the riot, and waxed deeply indignant about
the attack on the " Coombes." Soon, he
found—with much the same sort of surprise
with which Monk Schwartz or Roger Bacon
discovered gunpowder to be explosive—that

Adolphus Carter's name was being connected with the affair, and that he was passing from a feeling of utter incredulity about his share in the matter to a state of virtuous wrath against him for injuring an inoffensive stranger.   He next became conscious that he was, somehow, taking vast pains to connect Carter with Shelman and Shelman with the outbreak ; and, finally, that whatever information he had, respecting either of the two young men, was being heartily and effusively placed at the disposal of his dear friend, Mr. Edward—who had, he averred, been most shamefully treated—but how, he was not quite sure.

The little man, having taken his leave of Ned as though he were parting from his oldest friend for ever, made a bemused and ricketty progress home, and after a heavy sleep, from which his amazed landlady in vain tried to rouse him for his dinner—Timothy was a bachelor—awoke with very little idea of the main events of the morning's amusement— save that his indignation had gained him the most thoroughly business-like headache he had ever experienced, and that his mouth was very dry with over-much conversation.

But still, there remained stored up in his anything but lofty mind one fact, that somehow or other, he scarcely knew how—having regard to the deep affection for Ned that had suddenly seized him—it was incumbent on him to consider himself greatly affronted with both Carter and Shelman ; and when he had refreshed himself with cold water, eaten the late meal which had been saved for him, and slaked his thirst and steadied his nerves with a copious bowl of tea, he had fully settled in his mind that, without revealing the source of his knowledge, or betraying his new-found friend, he would make it his special business to reprove and punish—directly or indirectly, or, indeed, both—the conduct of the pair. Having made this resolution in the interest of friendship and the preservation of public and private morality, Mr. Rapsey sallied forth to spend the evening in his accustomed manner.

The next morning, as Alfred Shelman was leisurely eating his breakfast, Adolphus Carter was announced and entered to him in a state of great agitation. He waited until Shelman's man had retired and then said, in a tone little above a whisper :

"I say, Shelman, what on earth's to be done?"

"Done? what's the matter?"

"Last night," said Carter, wiping the cold perspiration from his brow, "I was coming home when I met little Rapsey. I've never seen him so before, but he was about half tipsy."

"Well?"

"He began to pitch into me about that—that row after the election. You know."

"Hang the election, and the row after it, too," said Shelman, angrily.

"Yes, yes, I know you must feel awfully worried over it—but I mean," said Carter, looking round nervously and glancing at the door—as though to make doubly sure that they were alone — "I mean about the 'Coombes' part of the business, you know."

"Curse the 'Coombes' and its owner, too," said the amiable Shelman.

"With all my heart," said Adolphus, his cheeks reddening; "I'm sure I bear him no good will. But do listen, for this concerns you."

"Me?"

"Yes."

" In what way ? "

" Why in this : Rapsey's found out, somehow or other—not through me, for I swear I've
never opened my mouth to a soul—that you
and I planned that affair together."

" Together;" said Shelman," take care what
you're talking about, young fellow.   Don't you
bring me into the affair, I warn you."

" Not bring you in ? " said Carter ; " why,
who proposed the whole thing ? "

" You did.   You came to me burning with
rage against the pair of fellows who live there
and swearing you'd be revenged on them both.
What had I to do with it ? "

" What had you to do with it ?   Why, just
as much as I had.   Didn't you say you hated
Galbraith yourself, and would like to do him
a turn for coming between you and Mrs. Stanhope about the house, and for buying the horse
you wanted ? "

" You   fool ;   if   the   man   bought   the
' Coombes ' was that any reason for my smashing the windows of it, or was I going to wreck
his house because he bid more for a horse than
I did ?   You'll accuse me next of getting up
the riot ? "

" And suppose I did," cried Carter in desperation, as he saw his ally preparing to secure his retreat ; " how far wrong should I be ? "

Cornered cowards sometimes make bold strokes. This was a bolder one than Shelman had bargained for. He tried to parry it by bullying.

" By G— ! " said he, starting up and advancing towards Carter, " if you dare to hint that I had anything to do with it I'll break every bone in your body."

" I don't care," said Adolphus, now fairly at bay ; " I won't stand this sort of life any longer ; you can't kill me anyhow, and I don't believe much in your thrashing me. You're not Galbraith, or that cursed nigger either, and if you put a hand on me I'll go straight to the Mayor and tell him all I know, and I know more than you think, too ; for one thing," he went on, seeing that the other made no attempt to approach him, " I know who keeps Mackerell's people now he's in gaol at Ridgetown. Aye, and more than that. I know——"

" Hush, you great ass," said Shelman, peevishly, but with an abatement of his violent manner ; " sit down and let us talk it over quietly. We don't want all the town to hear us. I was hasty, old man," he added, holding out his hand. " I know you're upset a bit, too, or you wouldn't talk like that, but you can't imagine how the whole affair has worried me. Here," he went on, ringing the bell, " let's have something in, and have a quiet chat over a pipe together. Bompas is away, I know, so your time's your own. And now tell me all about it."

When the servant had placed the desired fluids and tobacco, and cleared the breakfast things away, the two conspirators sat down together to smoke and to see how the land lay with them.

To tell the truth Alfred Shelman was supremely uncomfortable about the news his visitor had to give him. It was true that the riot had broken out in a great measure from an accidental circumstance, but there had been much in it that had been his doing, and it had been only by the employment of a good deal of tact and some considerable amount of money too that he had been able to close the mouths of two or three of the moving spirits among the rioters who had been committed to prison for their share in the work, and now, if the news were in Rapsey's mouth, he said to himself, it might as well be in the

town crier's ; so it was with more inward fear
than he cared to acknowledge that he listened
to Carter's narration of his interview with
Timothy.

That drink-valiant little man, returning
from the "Bear," slightly the worse for his
modest potations, taken on top of Edward's
morning offerings, had encountered Carter,
who was also homeward bound. Assuming an
air which he intended to be dignified, he had,
without mentioning the source of his intelligence, terrified Adolphus by the information
that he knew all about the source of the riot
and the attack on Galbraith's house. In his
sober moments, Timothy would never have
ventured to mention Shelman's name, nor had
he any real knowledge that the latter had been
concerned, but the two names were jingling
together in his brain, and it became impossible to separate them. In common with most
chatterboxes possessed of scanty information,
Mr. Rapsey drew liberally on his own imagination, and, partly aided by the ejaculations and
exculpations of the astonished and terrified
Carter, and partly by one or two lucky hits,
he succeeded in endowing that nervous youth
with a conviction that his crime and folly and

that of his associate were thoroughly known to Timothy, who, in some vague and undefined manner, meant to exact a stern penalty from each of them for it. Carter had barely enough presence of mind to extract from the proposed avenger his promise that he would see him on the morrow, and that he would take no steps meanwhile.

Such was the story which he now related to Shelman, who seemed almost as disturbed as himself.

Various means of securing their safety were discussed at the sitting, but two alone seemed to remain for choice : either to bribe the little man to silence or to frighten him into retraction. It is needless to say that it was Carter who suggested the former method, but it met with Shelman's opposition.

"The little beggar's got plenty of money for himself," said he ; "he banks with us, and I know his affairs to a penny. He's had about three hundred a year—of course I'm telling this to you confidentially as we're in the mud together—ever since he was twenty-one, and although he's never done a stroke of work since he sold his business, he has never been extravagant in anything, and hasn't lived up

to more than half his income. He's not at all
greedy for money, for he could get a good deal
better interest in twenty safe things than we
pay him on his deposit account, and a good
many people would open their eyes if they
knew how much that was ; no, money in this
case isn't any good, strange to say, and you're
never safe in the hands of a man you bribe ;
we must ride the high horse, Carter, and
frighten him."

" How do you propose to do it ? "

" Send him a lawyer's letter, threatening an
action for slander."

" That'll frighten him. Whom will you get
to do it : not Sennett ? "

" Sennett—nonsense ! There are more law-
yers in the world than Sennett. Leave that
to me. If he broaches the matter again, defy
him, dare him to prove his words, and before
he has time to take any steps, we'll be down
upon him with our threat of action."

" Yes," said Carter, doubtfully, " I'll see him
at once."

" No, no," said Shelman, " don't go a yard
out of your way ; indeed, try if you can to
postpone any interview, without, of course, appearing to wish to avoid him. Together with

the lawyer's letter he'll get one from the Bank calling on him to withdraw his account, and in two days we'll have him on his knees."

With this pleasing hope the two parted.

As frequently happens when persons give reproofs and assume indignation under spirituous influences, Mr. Timothy Rapsey had no intention, when he woke on the morning after he had poured out his wrath on Adolphus Carter, of carrying the matter any farther; without having forgotten the occurrence, he had done with it and put it aside. On the third morning after his visit to Ned, on descending the street, he had just given the old postman his customary morning salutation, when that worthy, to his surprise, stopped him as he was passing.

"Hold on a minute, Mr. Rapsey; I've got two letters for 'ee."

"For me?" said Timothy; "two letters! Why, dear me, whoever can they be from?"

"Ah, that's moor than I do knaw," said the postman, grinning, "but here they be."

Mr. Rapsey took the letters, and, adjusting his spectacles to his nose, essayed to open them. He was awkward at it though, with one letter tucked under his arm, and the wind was too high for comfortable reading; so, placing both epistles in his pocket, he betook himself home to peruse them in comfort.

The first that presented itself to his astonished gaze was couched in these, to him, incomprehensible words :

> "84, Lincoln's Inn Fields,
> "London.

"Sir,—We are instructed by our client, Mr. Alfred Shelman, to enter an action against you for slander, in which our client lays his damages at one thousand pounds.

"The slander imputed consists in an accusation which you have thought fit to bring against Mr. Shelman, to the effect that he had conspired with another person to wreck and destroy, or cause to be so destroyed and wrecked, a certain dwelling-house, situate in Avonham, and called 'The Coombes.'

"We shall be glad to be favoured with the name of the solicitor who will act for you in this matter.

> "We are, Sir,
> "Your obedient servants,
> "BLACKWELL, RIDLEY AND GROVES."

To say that Timothy Rapsey was scared by the letter would be insufficient ; he was almost paralysed with terror. He read the missive twice and groaned over it dismally for some minutes, with the cold sweat of fear pouring from him. After some time, he remembered that there was another. He opened this, and read as follows :

" Avonham Bank.

" SIR,—We have to request that you will have the goodness to withdraw both your current and deposit accounts from this Bank, as we must decline any further transactions with you.

" We are, Sir,

" Your obedient servants,

" BOLDHAM, HUMBERSTONE,

BOLDHAM AND CO."

" Goodness gracious me," moaned poor Timothy ; " whatever shall I do ? "

He did the very last thing that his two would-be persecutors could have imagined. He sat for a few minutes to collect himself, and then, with a beating heart and a pale face, betook himself to the " Coombes."

It is a dangerous thing to over-terrify a weak man. Dangerous for the actor as well as the agent. The weak man is apt naturally to look for help, and he goes to the strongest help he knows of. In place of seeking the advice of his friend Sennett, Rapsey determined to find Galbraith and lay his trouble before him. His house was the cause of the trouble, he argued, and in his house had he conceived the unlucky notion which had led him into this scrape.

Mr. Adolphus Carter happened to catch sight of the poor terrified little man, as with trembling limbs and bloodless face he went past Mr. Bompas's office window in South Street. It was a welcome spectacle to him, for Bryceson had, a few minutes before, driven past with a stranger by his side, and Mr. Raraty seated at the back of the dog-cart. What a funk the little man looked in to be sure, thought Adolphus as Timothy passed down the street. This would teach him not to interfere with his superiors another time. His manner would be a little more respectful the next time they met. Adolphus was doubled up with laughter ; he went to the door to gaze after him.

But when he reached the step all trace of

laughter vanished out of his face in an instant, and he grew pale in his turn.

" Good gracious, what's he going in at the gate of the ' Coombes ' for ? " said he to himself.

Mr. Carter had not forgotten that Shelman knew absolutely nothing of his own capture, release, and pardon by Galbraith, and a horrible thought stole over him that Rapsey *did* know of it and would use the fact as a weapon of defence against Shelman. And they had not counted on resistance either.

Adolphus went back to his desk, smiling no longer.

Meanwhile, Rapsey had entered the gate and was tottering along the path to the door which he had entered so joyfully and quitted so jovially on the occasion of his last visit. At the door was Bryceson, talking to a stranger.

" Good morning, sir," said he timidly, and his voice sounded hollow and faint, and unlike his own in his ears.

" Good morning, Mr. Rapsey," said Bryceson cheerily ; " what brings you this way ? What can we do for you ? "

" I was wishful, if you please, sir," said poor

Timothy, "to speak to Mr. Edward, if I might take the liberty."

The terrified little man was quite beaten down by his trouble.

"Ned has just gone over to Avonham Road for some luggage and things," said Bryceson. "Can I do anything for you till he returns?"

"I don't know, sir," said Timothy, with his eyes fixed and staring. "I'm in—in great trouble, sir—see Mr. Galbraith, sir—these—letters——"

And with these wandering words, and with a vain effort to take the letters from his pocket, he fell forward, fainting, into Bryceson's strong arms.

That afternoon, as Adolphus Carter was preparing to leave the office, a note was handed to him by one of the ostlers of the "Bear." He opened it and read:

"Bear Hotel, A'ham.

"DEAR SIR,—As I hear Mr. Bompas is absent from home, may I request an interview with you here at your earliest convenience, on important business?—Yours truly,

"FREDK. R. MARKHAM."

Greatly impressed with a sense of his importance, Carter at once proceeded to the "Bear," and on asking for Mr. Markham was shown upstairs to a private room. He waited alone for a minute or two, and then, the door opening, the stranger whom he had seen that morning seated by Bryceson's side entered, followed by Bryceson himself.

For the second time that day Adolphus turned pale, and his pallor was not diminished when Bryceson locked the door, and, pointing to a chair, said sternly :

"Sit down, Mr. Carter. I thought we had done with you the other night, but it appears not."

Adolphus Carter sat down and waited events in a state of agitation almost as great as that of his victim Timothy Rapsey.

CHAPTER VII.

THE MAKINGS OF A VERY PRETTY QUARREL.

In very truth the present position of Mr. Adolphus Carter was an unenviable one, and he mentally cursed his fate for having led him a second time into a contest with the inmates of the " Coombes." He sat white and shivering, looking first at Bryceson, who was leisurely sorting over a few papers which he had taken from his pocket, and then at Markham, who stood regarding him gravely and sternly. Adolphus almost wished himself back in the dining - room at the " Coombes," with the negro's strong grip on his arm.

There is a certain feeling which comes over the mind of a mean man when he is confronted with courage, integrity and rectitude of purpose, which is, perhaps, among the most painful of all the experiences that can happen to wrongdoers. That feeling is not one of hatred so much as of envy, not so much of malice as of admiration. Sitting there, awaiting his fate,

27—2

eagerly expectant of the opening words of a
speech and conversation the result of which he
could not foresee, he was as sincere an admirer
of the two young men who were about to apply
the torture to him as though he had been their
oldest friend.   What would he not give to be
able to stand in their position ?   How could
he have been so mad—he, a puny, weak-headed
frivolous fool, as he told himself he was—as to
engage in a contest with men who seemed to
him, as he thought of his own unworthiness,
like beings of a different sphere ?

Bryceson sorted his papers for a couple of
minutes, and selecting three from them, laid
them on the table and placed the others in his
pocket-book ; he then turned to Carter and,
speaking as though the matter in hand were
an ordinary business one, said :

"Mr. Carter, you know, of course, something of legal matters—of ordinary everyday
legal matters, I mean ?"

"Yes," said Carter, in a tone as brisk as he
could assume ; he would make what fight he
could of it, he told himself.

"You know what a power of attorney is ?"

"Oh, yes."

"This," said Bryceson, handing him the

topmost of the three selected papers, " as you will see, is a power of attorney from my friend, Mr. Henry Galbraith. authorising me to act in all matters for him during his absence."

Carter took the document handed to him and glanced over it, principally because it *was* handed to him, and he had no other course.

" Thank you, Mr. Bryceson," said he, returning it.

" I should have acted in this affair myself," said Bryceson, " even if I had not held this authority, but you will understand that as the matter stands I am now proceeding on behalf of my friend Mr. Galbraith ; not from any desire to avoid any responsibility, but because I am sure it is what my friend would have wished."

Adolphus inclined his head, having no words with which to reply.

" So much for the first paper, which I showed you as a matter of form," said Bryceson, " now for the second. Do you know a firm of solicitors in London named Blackwell, Ridley and Groves ? "

" No."

Bryceson and Markham exchanged glances.

" Do you know anything of this letter ? "

said Bryceson, handing him the document which had so terrified Timothy Rapsey.

The letter trembled in Carter's hands, as he read it. He felt strong indignation against Shelman for his utter want of tact in this action. This was a pretty way of bringing Timothy Rapsey to his knees in two days.

The letter took a long time in reading, short as it was ; the two friends remained silent, and Mr. Carter was uninterrupted ; his eyes were on the words, but after his first reading of them he saw them not ; he saw through them the angry brow of Shelman, the stern set features of Galbraith, the righteous wrath of Mr. Bompas, his father's grief-stricken face and his mother's anxious eyes. The silence grew painful to him, but he dared not break it. Faintly in the street he could hear Prosser, the bellman and crier, calling out some announcement ; he wondered what it was ; the clock above his head he noticed had a loud tick and a slight irregularity in it ; they had a clock at home something like it. Downstairs somebody laughed in the bar-parlour ; he felt angry with him for indulging in unseemly mirth ; how could anyone laugh at such a time ?

At last he laid the letter down on the table.

" I have never seen it before," he said.

" You misunderstand my question," said Bryceson, quietly ; " I asked you whether you know anything of it.   Do you ? "

For a moment or two Carter hesitated, but he felt the game was up ; he had played bad cards badly, and the odds were all one way.

" I knew it was going to be sent," he said.

" Thank you," said Bryceson ; " now we come to the last of the papers I have to show you just now."

He took the Bank letter and handed it to Carter.

" Do you know anything of *that* ? "

Hesitation was of no use now.

" I knew that was going to be sent, too," he said, and felt that he had indeed " burned his ships."

" It is a holograph, you will observe," said Bryceson.   " May I enquire whether you know the handwriting ? "

" I do," said Carter.

" Will you tell me whose handwriting it is ? "

" Mr. Alfred Shelman's."

" This other letter, of course, was sent at Mr. Shelman's instigation ? "

" It was."

" It mentions an accusation of conspiracy with another person ; did you notice that."

" Yes," said Carter faintly, for he felt that the crisis was coming now.

" I wanted to draw your attention to that for a special reason," said Bryceson ; "and now, Mr. Carter, I will tell you what you are perhaps a little curious to know, and that is how those last two papers came into my possession."

Carter murmured something inarticulate.

" Mr. Rapsey," said Bryceson, looking steadily at Carter, who quailed before his gaze, " of whom I know nothing whatever beyond what little I have seen of him about the town during my stay here, came to my friend's house, which I am at present occupying, this morning to see Mr. Galbraith's servant, whom I daresay you remember."

" Would he ever forget him ? " Carter thought.

" Mr. Rapsey," Bryceson went on, " seemed in trouble, and proved to be very much upset by the receipt of these two letters. He could only account for them in one way, and that was this. He and Edward had been gossiping together a few days previously, and amongst other topics they hit upon a certain little episode of the night of the election day, which I have no doubt you also remember. That evening Mr. Rapsey had a conversation with you upon the subject, I believe ? "

" Yes."

" And to that conversation he attributes, whether correctly or incorrectly, these threatening documents. Naturally he is much alarmed at them. Mr. Rapsey does not appear to be what you and my friend here would call a business man, and he does not seem to be possessed of the necessary strength of mind which enables gentlemen like yourself to become leaders of men in dangerous and sometimes unsuccessful night attacks and riots."

The " leader of men " looked anything but strong-minded as he moved uneasily in his seat, as though Bryceson's speech had been the lash of a whip descending on his back.

" Mr. Rapsey's first visit," said Bryceson, " was to Edward. Now, Mr. Carter, Edward is not an ordinary servant in any sense of the word. Since Edward has been in Mr. Galbraith's service, he has had a good many masters, first and last. Ned has been servant,

companion and friend—yes, *friend*, Mr. Carter.
—to Mr. Galbraith, to my friend here, Mr.
Markham, to me, and to three or four friends
of ours, of whom neither you nor anyone else
in Avonham knows, or is likely to know, anything. Mr. Rapsey, of course, was not aware
of this ; he went to Edward simply because
the conversation to which, as I say, he attributes these letters, occurred between them.
Very fortunately I happened to be in Avonham,
having arrived here this morning, and have
taken the matter in hand. This is the reason
of this meeting this afternoon. You will
excuse, under the circumstances, the little
scheme by which I was able to ensure your
presence here, and now having given you an
account of the matter so far, we will, if you
please, proceed to real business."

Fred Markham, as if to mark that a point
in the negotiations had been reached, took a
chair and seated himself astride of it with his
arms resting on the back.

"That business, Mr. Carter," pursued
Bryceson, still in the calm and quiet tone
which he had preserved from the commencement of the interview, "may be very much
simplified by you. No one knows so well as

you the cause of the attack on Mr. Galbraith's house. You were, according to your own confession to Mr. Bompas, the leader of the mob on that occasion. I cannot see that Mr. Galbraith has ever injured you in any way; and that it was a political matter is out of the question. It is perfectly evident to me that you were acting in concert with someone else, if not at his instigation. Now, Mr. Carter, we must know, if you please, who that person was."

Adolphus turned even paler than he had been before; he was between the devil and the deep sea with a vengeance.

"Suppose," he said, after a short silence, "that your surmise was wrong, and that it was entirely my own doing."

"We will not waste time by supposing anything so foolish, if you please, Mr. Carter," said Bryceson, quietly.

"But," said Carter, hesitatingly, "you don't know that I did not do it of my own accord."

"We have our own common sense in the matter, Mr. Carter, besides one or two little pieces of evidence which would perhaps surprise you if we used them. Do not, I beg of you, waste our time, although it is not specially valuable just at present ; let us know at once who inspired you with the idea of attacking Mr. Galbraith's house ? "

" It's not fair—it's not fair to ask me," broke out Adolphus in sheer desperation, and momentarily rendered courageous by the sense of his position : " it's not fair for two of you to get me in a room and lock the door and then torture me with questions ; you'll thrash me if I don't answer, I suppose ? " he said with a snarl ; " it's cowardly ! "

Bryceson's colour slightly rose, and he bit his lips before replying.

" You are as safe from violence here, sir," he said, "as though you were in your mother's arms, and I think you know it," he added pointedly. " Now let us distinctly understand each other. Do you refuse to give us, for our own satisfaction only—for we think we know it already—the name of the person who instigated the attack on the ' Coombes ? ' "

Carter paused again.

" Suppose I refuse to answer any question you put me ? " he said.

" We shall take very prompt measures to compel you to answer to someone else," said Bryceson.

"How?" said Adolphus, in a hoarse whisper, his lips and cheeks ashy white.

"In this way, Mr. Carter," said Markham, speaking for the first time. "We have strongly advised Mr. Rapsey to defend the action with which Mr. Shelman threatens him, and you will be a witness in that action on one side or the other, I venture to say. In addition to that my friend Mr. Bryceson will at once apply to the Mayor or the magistrates here for a warrant against you for attacking Mr. Galbraith's house. It is extremely probable, Mr. Carter, that you will give evidence in the slander case, attired in an unbecoming and not very honourable uniform. The whole of the questions my friend has asked to-day will be put to you then, and you will not be allowed the latitude that he has shown you in this room."

"But," said Carter, "what better shall I be off by telling you anything? If the action goes on I shall—so you say—be a witness, and obliged to tell."

"I fancy not," said Markham. "When my friend asked you just now not to waste our time, it was not merely our time in this room that he meant. You will distinctly understand that, as we shall have to deal with a second party, we cannot make any definite and binding promise about the matter, but if you supply us with the information we require—and really we only require it of you to confirm a suspicion so well founded as to be almost a certainty—I think that there will not be the slightest chance of the action being carried on, so that you need not dread your appearance in the witness box, nor need you fear any further proceeding against yourself on Mr. Galbraith's part, or on that of his representative ? Am I right in that last remark, Walter ? "

" Quite, Fred," said Bryceson.

Carter saw that at any rate there was a chance of safety from one of the dangers besetting him, and made up his mind to surrender.

" I must give way to you, Mr. Bryceson," he said, in a helpless tone ; " I will give up the name on those conditions."

" We can only make conditions with you for ourselves," said Bryceson ; " we cannot absolutely guarantee that the action for slander will not be pressed. Don't give us credit for anything but straightforwardness in the affair. You must take your chance so far as the slander is concerned."

"I must do that, I suppose. I am willing to give up the name of the person who got up the attack on Mr. Galbraith's house, and who set me on to do it."

"Who was it?" asked Bryceson.

"Mr. Alfred Shelman," said Carter.

"Thank you," said Bryceson; "he is just the person we suspected. Mr. Galbraith, whose judgment is about as keen as that of any man I have ever met, told me before he left Avonham that he imagined Mr. Shelman was at the bottom of it. Well, Mr. Carter, after your confession, I think it extremely improbable that you will be troubled to give any evidence in public. Of course," he added hesitatingly. "we may rely upon your—your information as being correct."

"Quite," said Carter, in a low voice, but with an evident sense of relief after his surrender.

"I don't want to ask you anything more compromising than the statement you have just made," said Markham, "but can you tell me what cause of quarrel this man Shelman had with Mr. Galbraith? So far as I can make out, they have never even spoken."

Carter had given up the name of his principal chiefly to place himself in a secure position

with regard to the two friends ; he was not
wholly displeased at the turn things had taken ;
it was obvious to him that if Rapsey's cause
were espoused by these young men it would
become a very strong one. and one that would
terrify even Alfred Shelman ; it was better,
perhaps, on the whole for him to enlist at once
on their side, at least so far as giving them all
the information in his power went, so he
replied :

"Mr. Shelman always had a feeling of irritation and jealousy against Mr. Galbraith ever
since he bought the ' Coombes.' "

" Because he wanted it himself, I suppose,"
said Bryceson.

" Yes, and he was disappointed by Mrs.
Stanhope's refusal to let him have the house
and land in preference to Mr. Galbraith," said
Carter, " and Mr. Galbraith bought a horse
that Shelman wanted, and——"

" And these," interrupted Bryceson, unconsciously using the very argument which
Shelman had himself advanced to Carter at
the meeting which had led to all this trouble,
" these are reasons for attacking a man and
making him the victim of an election riot !
Well, for an old-fashioned town with a three-

century-old charter, I must say you know how to play it down low on a tender-foot. Old Squire Gulch wasn't so very much ahead of this place in smartness, was it, Fred ? "

" Well, we'd Judge Lynch there for one thing," said Markham, " and upon my word his court wouldn't work badly here, I fancy. Pray, Mr. Carter, can you inform us, without very seriously compromising yourself, how *you* came to be selected as the instrument of this terrible man's vengeance ? "

If Markham had struck Carter he could not have roused him by the blow as he did by his question. Whether it was that he felt safe from bodily harm after Bryceson's assurance. or whether the sense of his injuries took away his reason and made him reckless of consequences, is not sure ; certain it is, however, that he broke forthwith into a rage which, without alarming either of his hearers, surprised them extremely.

" How ? " he screamed, " how ? Because I hate your friend ; haven't I enough cause to ? "

" To hate Galbraith," said Bryceson, astonished, " why——"

" To hate him, yes, and you too," shouted Carter, now quite beside himself.

" Me ? " said Bryceson, opening his eyes to
their fullest extent, and touching himself on
the breast to make sure that it was really he
whom Carter meant and no one else, " me !
Why, you fool, until the night after the election
I had never even spoken to you ; what reason,
in the devil's name, had you to hate me ? "

" Why did you come here at all ? " cried
Carter, foaming with impotent rage ; " I
never did a wrong thing in my life till Mr.
Galbraith came to Avonham ; my employer
liked me and trusted me, and would have taken
me into his business in course of time ; my
father was proud of me—yes, proud of me, and
with reason, for if I haven't your strength and
your good looks, and if I *am* in your hands
now, I'm not a fool at my business, or anything like one—and I was popular and respected
all over Avonham. What am I now ? I'm
in your power, and your friend has threatened
me just now with a jail and a convict's dress.
What does Mr. Bompas think of me now—or
my father ? You'll tell me that that change
came since the election row, and so it did ;
but I'd plenty of cause to hate you both before that. The very first words Mr. Galbraith
spoke to me were insulting, and I have never

forgotten them ; but there's more than that. If you want the real cause I'll tell you, and I don't care what you do to me afterwards— you may kill me if you like : since you came to this town I've never had a kind word from one of Mr. Bompas's daughters."

Markham gave a low soft whistle at this.

"I had plenty before, Mr. Bryceson ! Which of the girls it is you are after and which Mr. Galbraith wants I don't know, but I do know," he added, clenching his hands and tossing his arms with a gesture of supreme despair, "that you two have come between me and my love, and if my power had been equal to my will on election night you would have remembered it to the day of your death. *That* was the cause, if you want to know it ; and the scheme failed, and I'm ruined over it, and I curse the day you came into the town ! "

He had risen to his feet to say all this and stood facing the young men as a hunted beast turns for a last hopeless death-struggle. Bryceson and Markham remained seated, the former evidently greatly astonished by what he had heard.

Markham broke the short silence that followed.

" That's the secret of it, then ? Well, Mr. Carter, we're very much obliged for your frankness, and we have no wish to detain you any longer."

Carter seized his hat and turned to go.

" There is just one last word I want to say, Mr. Carter," said Bryceson, " don't you make any use of the names of those ladies in this town over this matter."

" No, I will not," said Carter, still hot, but with returning reason. " I'm not quite such a cad as that ! "

" I will take your word for it," said Bryceson, rising ; " and hope one day we shall be able to agree to forget this affair. I can't defend your conduct in your attack on my friend and myself—for I suppose I must include myself though I hadn't the remotest idea of it till now—but I'm less angry with you and more sorry for you than you think. Good day, Mr. Carter."

Carter opened the door and passed out, with a hardly audible reply to the salutation, and the friends were left alone.

" Well, Walter," said Fred, " that's an interesting young man ! It's a good job for human nature round here that that fellow hasn't an over-burden of pluck. He gives me the idea of a man whose malice is only bounded by his cowardice. If he had as much courage as he has spite, he'd make it nasty for his enemies."

"Harry's right; the dear old fellow has often told us never to despise a fellow because he's mean and weak. But I am sorry for him too. He'll come an awful cropper over this business."

"What did you think of his excuse for hating you?" said Fred; "complimentary to us, wasn't it, to be told that he might have had his pick of our lady-loves if you and Harry hadn't turned up? Of course he knows nothing about me and Lucy, but the principle's the same."

"It don't quite bear thinking of," said Bryceson; "well, I've shaped out my course with Shelman."

"He won't bring his action against that poor little man, will he?"

"I don't fancy he will, after I have done with him."

"Ned worked the little fellow beautifully, didn't he?"

"Splendidly. I must write to Harry about

it. I don't see yet any connection between this matter and the other, though."

"Nor I ; unless indeed this man Shelman has made it up with the widow, and she has set him on to Harry, suspecting who he is."

" You forget that she never saw Harry till he came to live here nor even heard his name ; he always went by Reginald's until he came to us."

"True ; I wonder whether she will recognise me ?—it may spoil all if she should. But I don't fancy she will. Ten years and more make a difference, and we weren't so *very* intimate after all. How carefully Harry followed her up."

" Yes, he did ; and if Reginald hadn't been discovered by the old Squire, I wouldn't have cared to stand in her shoes. Let us go downstairs."

Mr. Pinniffer and Mr. Barnabas Chickleholt were in the room when they entered, and both looked somewhat curiously at them. They had seen Carter's abrupt departure, for he had gone straight out into the street, looking white and ill, and without exchanging any greeting with anyone, and they wondered what was afloat. They got, however, no information out of the two friends, who drank a glass of wine together and left.

Carter quitted the house burning with a double rage—rage against both Bryceson and Shelman. By one he had been made a catspaw, by the other he had been treated as a cur. He felt that Bryceson must have been sure all along that he would divulge at once the name of his principal, and that he would betray him the moment pressure was put upon him. He *despised* himself for being a coward, but he did not *blame* himself. He even caught at the fact of his rage against Shelman as some sort of excuse for his having betrayed him to his enemies. But, over and over again, as he went on his way, he was vowing vengeance against all those whom he considered arrayed against him. Not only against Bryceson for having brought him to bay, and wrested his secret from him, but against Galbraith for having come to Avonham at all, against the Bompas family for having tolerated him, against Shelman for having attempted to interfere with him, against Edward for his suspicions, and Rapsey for his garrulity; he inveighed against them all. One thing he had made up his mind to do, and that was to have it out with Mr. Alfred Shelman as soon as possible.

He burst in upon that gentleman that evening as he was sitting at home, and broke into a storm of reproach and invective, which alarmed and surprised Shelman not a little. Incoherently he poured out upon him a jeremiad respecting their scheme, mixed with bitter lamentations for his own position, and warnings to him to avoid the fate which he had met. Shelman's was not the temper to allow him to sit patiently under such an outbreak.

"Sit down, curse you!" he shouted, "have you gone mad, Carter? Either give me a sensible account of what has happened, or stop your gibbering and get out!"

In presence of his ally Carter was a coward indeed. The idea that had possessed him after leaving the "Bear" had been first to up-braid Shelman and next to terrify him by an account of what he himself had had to undergo at the hands of the two men who had just put him on the rack. But Shelman was not a coward. He rose to the difficulty, and seeing plainly that his comrade had been terrified into divulging their secret, was determined to

extract from him the extent of his confession
in order that he might frame some plan
whereby he could avoid the consequences of
his own indiscretion and the cowardice of his
partner. Carter, as may be supposed, acted
as a weak mind will act when confronted with
a stronger one ; he partially recovered his
senses, and putting a strong restraint upon
himself was able to let Shelman know ap-
proximately how matters stood. It was Shelman's turn to get angry now ; he fairly boiled
over with rage and chagrin. For the third
time that day his cowardly associate was
panic-stricken ; he raved at him for his stu-
pidity, his bungling and his cowardice ; he
cursed Rapsey for his tale-bearing, and the
very existence of Galbraith, Bryceson, and the
opposite political party were sufficient ground
for him to indulge in a torrent of vituperation
against them. The way in which he vowed
vengeance against them almost persuaded
Carter that he was on the strong side after
all, and that this shouting, bullying, cursing
friend of his was a match for his opponents
yet.

But all his raving and raging, though it
relieved him, could not conceal from Shelman

the fact that he had been outwitted, and that his position was serious. He had compromised himself in several ways. He knew, though no one else did, the part he had taken after the election, and how much of the riot was due to him ; that was bad enough by itself. In addition to that, he had, on his own responsibility, and without the knowledge of his uncle, who was away from the town, ordered the closing of the accounts of a very good Bank customer, not anticipating for a moment that the said closing of accounts would ever be likely to occur, and he had threatened with an action for slander a man, who, instead of flinging himself at his feet and praying for mercy, had discovered, through his very weakness, friends who not only were prepared to resist him vigorously, but were in possession of a fact, which of itself justified the so-called slander. His political standing in Avonham and his position as a partner in the Bank seemed alike imperilled and threatened by those whom he most hated and despised.

It is probable that the dreams of both Carter and Shelman were troubled that night ; but at any rate the night watches brought consideration, and Shelman had something

like a plan in his head when morning came.
He had reflected that it was most probable
that Bryceson had obtained the information
respecting the riot simply with a view to use
it as a means of defending Timothy Rapsey
from the consequences of an action. Well,
the action would not be brought, of course,
and the necessity for using the information
having passed away, it was probable that it
would not be used. He would see Rapsey
himself at his house, and must make up his
mind to eat a little humble pie before him ;
his influence surely had not all faded in the
little man's eyes, and a little concession and
condescension would work marvels with Timothy. He would put the action and the Bank
affair straight, and thus remove two great
stumbling blocks out of his way ; and with
respect to other matters, he must take the
risk. Only, he told himself, and his blustering
of the night before had not blinded his eyes to
the fact, he must be careful how he went to
work, either now or at any future time, with
the young men at the " Coombes." Great as
was the opinion which he held of his importance and abilities, he was unable to shut his
eyes to the fact that those gentlemen seemed

to be armed at all points and to be men of no ordinary calibre whom it were better policy to leave entirely alone.

CHAPTER VIII.

THE morning commenced with a little game of
cross purposes. Two persons were much disappointed, too. In a small town like Avonham,
consisting, as we have seen, of one long main
street, a market-place, a churchyard, and two
side streets, to meet a man whom you want is
an easy matter, provided always that the man
is in town. The general mode adopted is this.
We will say, for example, that an Avonham
Smith, wishes to meet, for business purposes,
an Avonham Jones. Smith walks out in the
morning, and calls at Jones's house. Failing
to find him at home, he visits the office of
White, the shop of Black, and the hotel of
Robinson. To each of these citizens he con-
fides the fact that he wants to see Jones;
meeting two more acquaintances in the street
he delivers the same message "in case you
might see 'm." Then he trusts to chance and
his friends. Each of the latter tells a friend that

Smith wants Jones, and in half-an-hour's time half the town knows the fact. Jones will hear that Smith wants him for hours after he has seen him, and, grown callous by long custom, will forty times reply to the question, " Have 'ee seen Smith ? "

But these two persons, each of whom was seeking to find someone, did not employ this time-honoured and well-nigh infallible plan to-day. They had, it is true, reasons of their own for not doing so, but the consequence was that each was disappointed.

They were Alfred Shelman, whom, by this time, we know, and Mr. Jared Norton, cashier of the Avonham Bank, whom we have once seen.

Alfred Shelman's object was to see Timothy Rapsey ; Jared Norton's object was to see Alfred Shelman, and each, that morning, failed.

After a breakfast eaten rather more hastily than usual, Shelman entered the dog-cart which was waiting for him by his overnight order, and, driving past the just-opened Bank, turned into the side street past the churchyard, pulled up at the door of the house in which Mr. Rapsey lived, and asked to see him. " Mr.

Rapsey ain't at home just now, sir," said the landlady, with many curtseys and bobbings.

"Dear me, that's very unfortunate," said Shelman ; "will you tell Mr. Rapsey that I want to see him very particularly ? "

"Oh, yes, certainly, sir," said the dame.

"Ask him, will you, whether he will step up to my house and have a bit of lunch with me at one o'clock. You won't forget, will you ? "

"Oh, dear me, no, Mr. Shelman," said the landlady, highly gratified, for to lunch with Mr. Shelman was, in her eyes, to sit amongst the great ones, and she felt that the honour done to her lodger reflected on herself.

Disappointment number one !

Shelman turned and drove back to the Bank. He did not get down, but one of the clerks, a junior, came out with a letter, which he handed to him.   Shelman opened and read it.

"It is from Mr. Millard," he said.   "I am just going out to Beytesbury to see him. There is nothing else, is there ? "

"No, sir."

"Is Mr. Norton in ? "

"He has been, sir, and opened the letters, after which he went out immediately, saying

he should not be long. He gave us the letters.
There is nothing special in them, sir."

"Tell him I called."

" Yes, sir."

Shelman gave the reins to the horse and
bowled away, leaving behind him the man who
was seeking for him in great uneasiness of mind.

The cause of Mr. Norton's perturbation was
this : he was accustomed to open all letters
received at the Bank, with the exception of
those addressed specially to Mr. Boldham or
Mr. Shelman. The correspondence that morning had not been heavy ; the local farmers and
tradesmen, with whom the bulk of the business
lay, were fonder of transacting their affairs by
personal interview than by letter, but one of
the missives had greatly astonished him. Had
the spire of St. Hildegard walked into the Bank
and requested him to discount its weathercock,
he would have been scarcely more surprised
than he was by the receipt of a letter from
Timothy Rapsey, which stated that, in reply
to their (the Bank's) communication, he would
present himself at their establishment that day
for the purpose of withdrawing both his deposit
and current accounts, as requested. As requested ! Mr. Jared Norton called for the

letter-book ; there was no copy of any such letter ! He himself had heard nothing of the matter, and it surpassed anything in his experience. Mr. Rapsey, he reasoned, had banked with them for years and years, and was just the sort of customer with whom the country banker delights to do business, a man with an ever-growing deposit account, and one perfectly willing to accept the Bank rate of interest in lieu of investing elsewhere. It was incomprehensible to him ; perhaps Mr. Shelman might know something of it. He would not even wait for him to visit the Bank but would go and see him at once.

Now, had Mr. Norton informed one of his clerks where he was going, he would have been told that the gentleman of whom he was in quest had just driven past, but he kept his own counsel and turned into the main street as Shelman turned into the side one where Rapsey lived. When he reached Shelman's house the door was opened by a maid-servant, ignorant that her master had left home, for he had driven out the back way. He seated himself in the dining-room and waited fully ten minutes before the girl returned and informed him that she had discovered that Shelman had gone. Making his way back to the Bank, Mr. Norton, to his great chagrin, was made acquainted with the young man's visit, and retired to the Bank parlour lamenting his ill-luck in not catching him.

Disappointment number two !

Mr. Norton resumed his accustomed seat, and waited the course of events.

At eleven o'clock Timothy Rapsey entered.

The double burden of business which he did not understand, and a secret which he must not divulge, had changed the little gossip's cheery bird-like face into a countenance of sphinx-like mystery and direful portent. Jared Norton, who had known him for thirty years, stared at him in amazement.

"Will you step this way, Mr. Rapsey ?" said he, not giving Timothy an opportunity of stating his business before the clerks.

He led the way to the Bank parlour, where he gave the visitor a seat, and waited in great curiosity for his opening address.

"I suppose you got my letter, Mr. Norton ?" said Timothy.

"Yes, Mr. Rapsey, I did, and I was never more surprised in——"

" Surprised, Mr. Norton ! what, didn't you know of it, then ? "

" Not one word, my dear sir, not one word, I assure you," answered the cashier.

" Well," said Timothy, taking a paper from his pocket, " there's the letter that brought me here, Mr. Norton ; maybe you know who sent it."

Norton gravely perused the letter, which we have already seen, and handed it back to its owner.

" It is correct enough, Mr. Rapsey," said he, " although I knew nothing of it, and I'm very sorry to see it now."

" I've banked here a good many years, and never thought to be served this way," said Rapsey, ruefully ; " but," he added, perking himself up like a bantam cock, " I ain't under no obligation to the Bank so far as I can see, and 'tis your loss, not mine."

" But, dear heart alive, Mr. Rapsey," said Norton, " is it well to fall out with us like this ? Why——"

" Now, Mr. Norton, I put it to you. Is it fair, after that letter, to say as I've fell out with you ? "

" Well, well, perhaps not, Mr. Rapsey ; but

won't you see Mr. Shelmam himself about it
when he comes in ? "

" Mr. Shelman was round to my place this
morning, about an hour ago, and I was out."

" Why, that must have been whilst I was
looking after him about this very matter, Mr.
Rapsey."

" 'Tis likely. Mr. Shelman leaved a message
to my house for me to come up and have
lunch with him at one o'clock, d'ye see, Mr.
Norton ? "

" Why, that's right," said Jared, much relieved, " that's right ; you can talk it——"

" Ah, but look 'ee here see, Mr. Norton,"
said Timothy, emphasising his words with his
forefinger on the palm of his other hand, " I
won't go, y' know ! "

Jared stared.

" Mr. Shelman," said Timothy, with the
same finger and palm play, " have a-threatened
me with an action——"

Jared started and stared yet more.

" And Mr. Shelman have written to me,"
pursued Timothy, " for me to draw all my
money away. Now, Mr. Norton, I b'ain't going
to be put upon by Mr. Shelman, n'yet no one
else, and so, as it sims likely as I shall want

my money to pay law expenses, I'm come for
it now, according to this letter."

Mr. Norton shook his head regretfully, but
saw no solution of the difficulty.

"Will you take the money now, Mr. Rapsey ?" said he.

"If you please, Mr. Norton. You've got
my pass-book, and I've brought my deposit
note and cheque-book, and if you'll let me know
what I'm to draw for, I'll do't at once and
take all away together."

Jared Norton gave up the business of per-
suasion in despair. The whole thing was, so
far as he was concerned, wrapped in mystery,
and quite outside his banking experience. He
sent for the book, and carried out the calcula-
tions necessary for a final closing of the accounts. Having done this with the air of a
martyr, he informed Timothy of the amount
standing to his credit in their books under
both heads.

Timothy produced his cheque-book with an
air of great dignity and proceeded to fill in the
partly-written cheque which he had prepared
for the occasion. It was a tolerably large sum,
and, annoyed as he was, the little man could
not resist a feeling of satisfaction as he wrote

the three figures after the £. Not many men
in Avonham, he thought, as he gazed com-
placently at them, would write such a cheque
for one sum at once. But the amount on
deposit, all of which Mr. Rapsey asked for in
notes, was something to look complacent over.
Shelman had not spoken lightly when he told
his confederate to what state of comfort Mr.
Rapsey's frugality had brought him.

He left the room and went to the front
office of the Bank itself to receive the notes.
As Norton finished counting the amount of
the current account, Mr. Beadlemore Arto
entered with a cheque. He shook hands with
Timothy, gave " good day" to the cashier and
clerks, and stood waiting his turn.

Mr. Arto was not curious—oh, dear, no !—
but he was not unwilling to notice, and Mr.
Rapsey was not unwilling that he should
notice, the amount which he received. Mr.
Arto opened his eyes but said nothing.

Jared Norton then, with a face full of un-
utterable things, handed solemnly to Rapsey a
second sheaf of notes, and held out his hand
for Mr. Beadlemore Arto's cheque. That
worthy's eyes were dilated to their fullest
extent as he noted the sum that his crony was

telling over. When he had counted them
twice, Timothy put the notes carefully into a
large envelope which he had brought with
him, and, placing this in his breast pocket,
carefully buttoned both his inner and outer
coats, and bade Mr. Norton and the clerks
good-day. Mr. Arto received the money for
the cheque which he presented and followed
him out.

"Where be goin' to ? " was his salutation.

"Up to Chris Raraty's," replied Timothy.
"I want to see 'm."

"He's over to Pinniffer's," said Arto. "I
see him goin' in as I went into th' Bank just
now."

"Ah, I do want him to let me have a trap
to drive over to Ridgetown on a bit o' business,"
said Timothy.

"Be 'ee goin' to buy the place, Timothy
Rapsey, that ye're taking all that cash over
there with 'ee ? T'ood be worth anyone's
while to foller and stop ye on the road," said
Mr. Beadlemore Arto, laughing at his own wit.

"No, I'm not," said Timothy, his face
lowering in spite of the comfortable feeling of
the notes in his pocket. "I've been and
drawed all my money out o' Boldham's Bank,

and I'm goin' over to Ridgetown to put it in the North Marlshire."

" Drawed all yer money out o' Boldham's ! " said Beadlemore Arto, stopping in his surprise and staring hard at Timothy, as though he were demented ; " why, what in the name o' sense and patience did 'ee do that for ? "

" I were told to," said Timothy.

" Why, who upon earth told 'ee ? " asked Beadlemore, still staring, if anything, wider than ever.

" I mustn't tell 'ee," said Timothy, the sense of his secret again weighing on him. " Now, don't ask me ; I really can't tell 'ee ; 'tis a secret, and don't for pity's sake say anything about it ! "

Mr. Beadlemore Arto resumed his progress, and the pair entered the familiar room together and found their cronies assembling pretty much as usual. Mr. Raraty was, as had been said, amongst the company, and Mr. Rapsey was not an hour older before, seated in a dog-cart behind a good-looking but steady-going mare, belonging to that gentleman, he was well on the way to Ridgetown. He left behind him in Avonham a very thoughtful and puzzled man in Mr. Arto.

That worthy pondered deeply over the words which Timothy had let fall. Whence he got his information (for he had no idea of the real state of the case, nor dreamed that the Bank authorities, or one of them, at least, had told him to withdraw his account) he could not imagine ; it was sufficient for him that it had been done under his eyes, and that there was a screw loose somewhere. Was it with the Bank ? Mr. Arto's transactions in corn, hay, oats, and straw were many, and his standing balance was not large in proportion to his trade ; nevertheless, it was large enough to make him feel uneasy about it in the face of what he had seen. He went home, took out his cheque-book and drew a cheque which reduced his balance to a very small sum indeed. He took it into the Bank with an excuse ready : a contemplated cash purchase on a large scale ; he had sometimes had to do so before. Norton heard his explanation, made no comment, but paid him the money cheerfully enough. In half-an-hour, Mr. Follwell came in and drew five hundred pounds : this was unusual. Following closely on his heels came Wolstenholme Pye, who was going to Bristol market on the next day, it appeared, and who also presented a heavy cheque. These were succeeded by ex-Mayor Killett, Mr. Pollimoy and Mr. Barnabas Chickleholt, who all appeared constrained in their manner, and were armed with cheques for somewhat abnormal amounts, made payable to "Self." By one o'clock, Mr. Norton was getting a little fidgety. There was nothing like a run on the Bank, and, knowing the resources he had at hand, he felt that even had that happened no real harm could come to such a steady and solvent establishment. But his experience told him that, setting Timothy's matter aside, this was the heaviest morning's draw he had ever had on a non-market day, and he shrewdly guessed that news of the transaction of the morning was circulating among the particular circle to which Mr. Rapsey was especially affiliated, that a mistaken idea of its nature had arisen, and that a wind of suspicion was beginning to blow on the credit of the Bank. He despatched an urgent note to Alfred Shelman, begging him to come to the Bank at once on most important and pressing business.

Shelman's errand that morning had been to Beytesbury to complete with Mr. Millard the arrangements for the purchase of the land belonging to the latter, which Shelman wanted for his new house.   All the points in question having been amicably discussed, and actual signature and transfer of deeds and payment of money being alone necessary to finish the business, Mr. Millard had returned to Avonham with Shelman, and had proceeded to the office of his friend Sennett to give him final instruc-tions.   Alfred had meanwhile gone to his house in the expectation of being shortly and punctu-ally waited upon by Timothy Rapsey, whom a little condescension and a little champagne would reduce to a peaceable and forgiving con-dition.   To his surprise, however, Timothy had not been seen, and, in the midst of his wonder at his absence, Norton's message came ; he immediately proceeded to the Bank, expecting nothing more important or pressing than that his signature was required for some special piece of business.

Old Norton met him, wearing an anxious appearance, which he noticed as he passed through the front office.

" What's the matter, Norton ? " he said, as he seated himself in a chair in the parlour, whither the cashier followed him.

"I am glad you have come, Mr. Alfred," said Norton; "I was getting rather anxious without you. I have had a very heavy morning."

Alfred Shelman did not answer, but awaited the business for which it had been deemed necessary to summon him.

The old cashier waited a moment for him to speak; but, receiving no reply, went on:

"Mr. Rapsey has been here this morning, sir."

"Ah!" said Shelman, suddenly evincing an interest in what was going forward.

"I tried to see you at ten o'clock," said Norton, "but we unfortunately missed each other. I got a letter from Mr. Rapsey, in answer to one from this office, informing us that he would call and remove his accounts, as requested in our communication. Mr. Alfred, there is no trace of that letter in the copying book, and, of course, I know nothing of it."

"No, no, I know," said Shelman, hastily. "I wrote it myself and did not copy it—well, what did Rapsey say? I invited him to lunch to-day, to talk the matter over; I suppose he didn't get the message in time."

"He got the message, Mr. Alfred," said

Norton, hesitatingly, " but—but he told me
that he—he should decline to accept the invi-
tation."

" He did ? " said Shelman, and his face
assumed a disturbed appearance.

" He seemed very determined in the matter,
and spoke of some action which you were
bringing against him," said the old cashier,
with a questioning look which Shelman did
not regard, " and finally he drew a cheque for
his current account, and withdrew his deposit
as well."

Shelman sprang to his feet with an oath, as
the consequences of his folly flashed across
him.   He would have a pretty quarter of
an hour with his uncle when he came to hear
of it.

" Of course I had no alternative in the face
of your letter but to give him what he
demanded," said Norton, " and I paid him.   I
fear that is not the worst of it."

" What else is there ? " said Shelman.

" Why, Mr. Alfred." said Norton, lowering
his voice and approaching nearer to Shelman,
" I fear that some mischief may follow.   Mr.
Arto was here when I was paying Mr. Rapsey,
and they went out together.   Not very long

after Mr. Arto came back and drew a good round sum, and soon after that Mr. Follwell had five hundred pounds ; since then we have had Mr. Pye, Mr. Killett, Mr. Chickleholt and Mr. Pollimoy, all drawing, all cheques to 'Self,' and all almost down to the lowest possible balance. I don't like the look of it, sir. They're all friends of Mr. Rapsey and all in one clique, and it's hard to say what rumours may get about in this place. It's not a good town to keep a secret in and we may have a run upon us at a moment's notice."

The old fellow looked grave ; Shelman alarmed.

"But we've nothing to fear from that," said the latter, after a moment's thought. "We could pay every current account five times over."

"If I didn't know that," said the elder man, smiling, "I should be worse upset than I am. But a run never did a bank any good yet, sir, and never will. People may say that the fact of standing against a run is a good advertisement, but I doubt it. There are always plenty of people who'll declare you only pulled through by the skin of your teeth ; most of them are outsiders, it's true, who never had a banking account in their lives, but talk's talk, and it tells ; and, then again, you'll always find you lose two classes of customers after a crisis ; those who are afraid of you, and those who are ashamed of themselves for having doubted you, and don't like to come back to you. No, Mr. Alfred, I'm not *afraid* of a run, but I don't want to see one, and whatever this matter is with Mr. Rapsey and you, I'm very sorry it ever occurred, and I hope it's not gone so far but that it can be put right."

The old man spoke firmly and looked as if he were uncertain how his words would be taken. Shelman, however, was too keen not to see that he was talking sound common sense, and he received the counsel readily.

" You're right, Norton ; the fact is I've been over hasty with Rapsey about an election matter, and I thought to give him a bit of a scare—that's all, upon my word—and he has taken the matter more seriously than I thought he would." And he explained to Norton the circumstances of the case.

" Law's a funny thing to play with," said the cashier, when he had heard the tale ; " take my advice, Mr. Alfred, make the matter right with Rapsey, and get his accounts back here again. It'll be better for all parties, I'm sure."

"I will take your advice, Norton," said Alfred Shelman; "I'll see the little ass at once. You needn't fear," he added, laughing; "I won't treat him roughly. I'll smooth him down the right way."

"I hope you may, sir," said Norton; and he returned to his duties whilst Shelman took his hat and quitted the Bank in search of Timothy Rapsey.

Mr. Rapsey was not at home, for the second time that day; his landlady was quite concerned that Mr. Shelman had missed him again; perhaps, she added, Mr. Shelman, if he didn't mind going there, might find him at the "Bear."

To the "Bear" then, he directed his steps.

That famous hostel filled, as will doubtless have been observed, more functions than that of providing good cheer for the wayfarer; it was the Exchange of Avonham, the local Parliament House or talking-shop of the place, and half the business of the town was transacted under the vaulted roof of its ancient gateway or in its spacious panelled rooms. Quarterly sessions, revising barrister's courts,

tolzey and brewster sessions, leet juries—all
had had, in past times, their headquarters at
the " Bear ; " and down to our own day was
held under its gateway, on Great Cheese market day, one of the most curious remnants of
bygone times, a court of *pie poudre*, which
does not, I believe, survive anywhere, but made
its appearance even down to a recent date once
a year in the Broadmead at Bristol. So that
even so mighty an Avonham potentate as Mr.
Alfred Shelman lost none of his dignity in
repairing to the great meeting-place of the
town in search of another citizen.

But, important as was his business, he little
guessed what would be the termination of his
visit there that day.

The first person whom he saw was Miss
Pinniffer, seated at the window of the bar,
brave in lilac poplin and cherry-coloured
ribbons. In answer to his queries, Miss
Pinniffer informed him that Mr. Rapsey was
not there—had gone out driving somewhere.
Mr. Raraty was in the parlour and could tell
him where, no doubt. Shelman opened the
door of the apartment and walked in ; as he
did so, he heard from the lips of Mr. Barnabas
Chickleholt, who was gruffer than usual, the

closing words of some oracular sentence that he had evidently been favouring his cronies with, about matters at the Avonham Bank.

"——to look after his own interest, and, break or not break, I'm very glad as I'm on the right side of the hedge myself. They're welcome to what I've left them."

Jack Rann took up his parable in a tone of some excitement.

"I believe——" he cried.

What Mr. Rann's creed on the point under discussion was will, perhaps, never be known; for events crowded so thickly on the enunciation of its first two words that it was never finished. Shelman entered the room, and Mr. Rann's mouth closed with a nervous snap.

Shelman took no notice of any of the words which he had heard, although he had some difficulty in restraining himself; he looked smilingly round the room and gave as near an approach to a cheery "Good morning, gentlemen," as was possible from one of his unamiable temperament.

"Good morning, sir," replied the room, not without a sense of guilt upon those who had just been discussing the very man whom they were saluting.

"Can I have a word with you, Raraty ? " said Shelman.

"Certainly, sir," said the post-master, rising from his seat with alacrity and advancing to the door.

"Do you know where Mr. Rapsey has gone to ?"

"He's taken one of my dog-carts, and gone to Ridgetown," said Christopher Raraty.

"Ah," said Shelman, "I wanted to see him before he went, but presently will do as well ; would you be good enough, if you should see him when he returns, to tell him I should like to have a word with him up at my house ?"

Mr. Raraty promised to convey the message.

It was Shelman's object to remain a few minutes in the room, quite at his ease, partly with a view of reassuring the minds of the assembled friends, all of whom he saw were customers of the Bank, by his appearance of unconcern, and partly to offer any one of them an opportunity of speaking to him on the subject which he knew was uppermost in each man's mind, in order that he might be able, without appearing to volunteer any information, to set at rest any doubts which might have arisen respecting the stability of his firm.

30—2

He stood and sipped a glass of sherry and chatted with one or two, but his object was defeated ; his questions were answered, but no more—a chill seemed to have fallen on the room and an uneasiness in his presence, coupled with an absolute disinclination to talk, totally foreign to the nature of the gathered cronies in the company of one of their local great ones. On an ordinary occasion he would have had everyone to reply to ; topics of all kinds would have been started for the sake of getting his opinion or his criticism, and little Timothy Rapsey would have been present as collector-in-chief of all his sayings, and snapper-up of all the trifles of his conversation which might appear likely to be of service at any future symposium. But now the little man whom he had barely tolerated, except at the Bank, and whom he had looked upon merely as an animated puppet who occasionally made him smile, was all in all to him, and his absence meant he knew not what evils and dangers, while the rest of the men sat silent and glum, with a silence and a glumness that were almost threatening. He soon ceased the attempt to engage anyone in connected conversation and stood moodily drinking a second glass of wine, for which he had called, in his usual sullen manner.

When he had finished this, he laid down the glass and a shilling beside it on the half-door of the little bar which communicated with the parlour, and went out, bestowing a parting salutation on the company as gruff and un-gracious as Mr. Barnabas Chickleholt could have feigned, and with an ill-temper very foreign to the nature of that grim personage, who like another and more celebrated man had nothing of the bear about him except the skin.

The conversation did not at once re-com-mence. Shelman had left the room but not the hotel, as they could hear his voice in the passage in conversation. John Rann was the first to break the silence.

"Well, that don't seem very much like anything being wrong with the Bank, Mr. Chickleholt," said he, in a low tone.

Rann, who had been one of the strongest partisans of Mr. Boldham at the election, had constituted himself the champion of the Bank at this juncture and had, previous to Shelman's entry, been ridiculing the idea of any suspicion of its solvency and stability.

"No one have said in my hearin'," growled

Barnabas, "as there was anything wrong with the Bank."

"No, no," said Wolstenholme Pye.

"Oh, dear, no," chimed in Hoppenner Pye.

"Well, you're mighty particular about terms, I think," said the market clerk.

"A man has to be keerful nowadays what 'a do say," chimed in the Nestor of Avonham, old "Mas'r Killett."

"'Bliged to be," said Hoppenner Pye, turning to Rann, as though to apologise for Chickleholt.

"Forced to be," said Wolstenholme Pye.

Rann leisurely finished the loading of his pipe, struck a villainous sulphur match which made Hoppenner Pye splutter and his brother cough, waited for the flame to brighten and applied it to his pipe before replying.

"If *(puff)* what we were *(puff)* saying about the Bank just *(puff)* now wasn't talking *(puff)* against it," said he, "I'm no judge o' plain speakin', that's all. Look here, Mas'r Killett," added he, pointing the smoking end of the match at the old oracle ; "how many years have this very Bank been in this very town and in the hands of the same families ? Tell me that, Mas'r Killett, will 'ee ?"

" Whoy," said the old man, taking his pipe from his mouth, pulling down his waistcoat, rubbing his leg and pointing with his yard of clay, " there ain't noo one alive as could mind the start of it. I'm the eldest man to Avonham, 'ceptin', p'rhaps, Daddy Prosser's father, and he'm a dotin' even if 'a *be* as old as what I be, and I can't mind it. I'll tell 'ee what, tho'! Lookee you all here, now, and see what I do say, for it's true if I nevermore move out o' this here cheer. My granfer * held hees money in't, that 'a did, an' 'a many yeers afore I were bore too, that 'twere. See that, now !"

" That's a very many years ago," said Wolstenholme Pye, reflectively.

" That goes back years and years," Hoppenner assented.

" Ah, you're right there, both of you," said John Rann, with a half sneer, as though to imply that it was an unusual matter ; " and do you mean to tell me——"

Rann's question shared the fate of the belief he was enunciating before Shelman's entry, and was never advanced a stage farther than its commencement, for the sound of voices, loud

* Grandfather.

in anger outside, broke in upon the low-toned conversation and checked it in a minute.

" Dear heart alive ! " said Mr. Beadlemore Arto, looking round the room in amazement, " why, whatever's to do ? "

The angry voices grew angrier and louder, and Miss Pinniffer who, within her bar, had risen to her feet in evident alarm, gave a frightened scream, called out some few words in an appealing tone, and rang violently at the bell which communicated with the back of the hotel. Wolstenholme Pye, who was sitting close to the window, got up and looked out with a loud, " Lawks a daisy how ! " and flung the sash up, thrusting out his head, and as much of his body as he could with safety get through. Rann dropped his pipe, which shivered to pieces on the floor, and Barnabas Chickleholt, who was nearest the door, threw it open and rushed out into the passage followed by all in the room, except the Pyes, who fraternally shared the window. The sight that met their eyes was enough to rouse all Avonham.

When Alfred Shelman had taken his un-gracious farewell of the inmates of the parlour of the " Bear," and closed the door behind him, the first person who met his view as he stood moodily in the passage was our light-hearted friend Walter Bryceson, who was just mounting the stone steps, accompanied by Mr. Millard, with whom he was laughing and talking, and Fred Markham.

The fun went out of Bryceson's face the moment he saw Shelman ; he had not expected to meet him just then, but his mind was made up with respect to him, and he determined to bring him to book at once. Shelman was not known to Markham by sight, and Mr. Millard was, of course, unconscious of anything wrong.

As Shelman was about to pass out at the front door with an ordinary greeting to Mr. Millard, whom he had not long ago left, Bryceson stepped right in his path and brought him perforce to a standstill.

" A word with you, if you please," said he, sternly, laying his left hand on Shelman's shoulder.

" On what subject, sir ? " replied Shelman, haughtily stepping back, and shaking himself free of the other's hold.

" On two, sir," said Bryceson ; " on your plot to wreck my friend Galbraith's house the other night and on your threatened action for slander against Mr. Rapsey."

" And what the devil business have you with either the house or Rapsey ? " said Shelman, hotly, as he endeavoured to pass out.

" Just this," said Bryceson, " as I happened to be in the house when your vagabonds attacked it——"

" My vagabonds ! " cried Shelman. " How dare you speak to me in this way, sir ? What do you mean ? Stand out of my path, or I will stop your insolence in a way which you won't like ! "

" I mean exactly what I say, sir," said Bryceson, " and it'll take a better man than you to stop me. As I was just as likely to suffer as my friend, that part of the affair is my business, and as I intend to interfere between you and Mr. Rapsey on account of a certain interest I have in the matter, that's my business too ; at any rate, I choose to make it so. Now, sir, just explain your conduct in the first matter, will you ? "

Mr. Millard had listened to this conversation with feelings which it would be hard to describe. He now interfered.

" Mr. Bryceson—Mr. Shelman—for goodness' sake—what does this mean ? Gentlemen, I beg of you to be calm."

"I'll tell you what it means," said Bryceson, answering the question, but by no means acceding to the request. "You were over at our place a little while ago concerning a certain young captive whom we took on the night of the election—allow me to introduce you to his employer," and he indicated Shelman.

"Do you mean to insult me ?" shouted Shelman, beside himself with rage. "Let me pass, or——"

"What will you do ? Do you think you are dealing with little Rapsey, you bully ? Do you know that we've your confederate's confession ? You scoundrel, I believe the whole of the work of that riot was your doing !"

"You are a liar !" yelled Shelman ; "stand out of my way."

"I won't !" said Bryceson, as much roused as the other.

"Take that, then," shrieked Shelman, and dashed his fist at the other's face.

Short but fierce was the fray that followed. Both were powerfully made young men, in the very prime of manhood, Shelman half mad

with rage and Bryceson roused in an unusual
degree.　But the latter was the stronger and
the more skilful, and when the first half-dozen
hot, wild, uncalculated slogs had passed, Shelman, who, with all his faults, had not a par-
ticle of physical cowardice in his composition,
discovered that he was unable to make any
impression on his foe, and that he himself was
being desperately punished.　Three times was
he hit back against the wall, the narrowness of
the place in which they were fighting preclud-
ing a knock down blow ; at last he managed
to shift his position, and trusting to the moral
effect of a rush he dashed in to drive his enemy
before him, but was twice hit back again by
Bryceson's left, and, rushing in a third time
with head down, hoping to be successful with
the goat-like tactics of the late Edward Stock-
man, Esq., a distinguished and refined member
of the Prize Ring, better known to fame as the
" Lively Kid," he was met with a fearful upper
cut and a straight hit from his opponent's right
that knocked him down in a huddled-up mass
at the bottom of the " Bear " steps.

The scene that followed was as exciting as
any in the annals of the town.　When the
paralysis of surprise was over, half a score

persons, headed by Pinniffer and ex-Mayor
Killett, threw themselves between the combatants and prevented any further contest for
the present.   Bursting through the crowd that
had speedily collected came the negro Edward,
with a war-gleam in his rolling eyes and a
display of teeth that was diabolical in the eyes
of the youths who flocked to the spot.   The
hubbub that rose was fearful.   Mr. Millard
was endeavouring to make peace, the spectators
all talking at the top of their voices, the negro
assisting his present master, Markham threatening a friend of Shelman's who had uttered
some words derogatory to Bryceson, and the
combatants themselves on the point of renewing the battle in spite of the well-wishers, who
were respectfully but firmly endeavouring to
prevent it.   In the midst of all this Mr. Sennett, the Mayor, came upon the scene and
forced his way into the middle of the crowd.

" What is the meaning of this, Millard ? "
he asked.

" God knows ! " said the astonished Millard.
" I don't ! "

" Gentlemen, have you taken leave of your
senses ? " cried the Mayor.

Neither foe replied, but such obviously hos-

tile preparations for renewing the fray went
forward that the Mayor's temper was roused
by the disregard of his authority.

"Mr. Shelman and Mr. Bryceson," he cried,
"if you do not instantly cease this disgraceful
struggle and depart quietly, I will issue my
warrant against each of you for a breach of the
Queen's peace, and imprison you both ! I call
on all present to assist me in the Queen's
name ! "

The sturdy old fellow meant what he said,
and a murmur of respect went up from the
crowd. Bryceson and Shelman scowled at
each other fiercely, and, if the truth must be
told, a little melodramatically ; then Markham,
seizing Walter's arm, pushed through the crowd
with him and entered the " Bear," followed by
the negro. Shelman, bleeding profusely from
the face, and already sick and faint from the
fearful blows he had received, was supported
across the market-place towards his home by
Killett and one of the bank clerks who had
been present at the row.

How many venerable and respectable heads
were shaken over the news, how many pipes
were smoked over it, and from how many
points the fight was discussed, would be hard

to say. Two persons in Avonham, besides the principals, each of whom next morning was somewhat ashamed of the affair, were in a sad state of mind over the matter. One was Adolphus Carter, who could see nothing but harm to himself ensuing from the occurrence ; the other Timothy Rapsey, who paraded the town like a discontented bee, extracting from every possible source the countless descriptions of the combat that were flying about the town, and after every fresh piece of information exclaiming, with heartfelt and sincere regret :

" Oh, deary me, deary me, what a misfortune, to be sure ! Oh dear, oh dear, why ever wasn't I there ? "

CHAPTER IX.

THE MURMUR OF THE HIVE.

NESTOR in his long and honoured life must have met with novelty in the minds of men. We may fairly imagine that he would sometimes shake his venerable head over the changes that were taking place in his latter days. Certain it is that his representative in Avonham, Master Killett, was compelled to own that he had never known such all-absorbing interest shown in the town of which he was the Nestor as was displayed over the encounter between Bryceson and Shelman. There was no getting a word in on any other subject next market day. Every farmer who attended market had to be regaled with the news ; fifteen different reasons were assigned for the quarrel ; partisans were not wanting for both sides, and the town was in a ferment. Those highly favoured individuals who had been fortunate enough to be actual eye-witnesses of the combat itself found their company more eagerly sought after

than on any other market day in their recollection. Generally speaking, they were to be
found in a group together somewhere in the
immediate neighbourhood of the battle-field,
for it was deemed almost indispensable to the
proper telling of the tale that the listener should
have pointed out to him the actual spot on
which the meeting took place, the very steps
down which Shelman had been propelled, the
exact square of stone on which Bryceson had
stood when he delivered his last and most
effective blow, and the precise course which the
Mayor had taken when he bore down upon the
combatants and prevented the affray from
going any further. So that the gateway of
the " Bear," always the busiest spot in the
town on market day, was more thronged than
ever, and from early morning till late in the
afternoon the battle was fought again.

Attached in some mysterious manner to the
history was a rumour that there had been
some suspicion in the minds of some of the best
men in Avonham as to the Avonham Bank.
Norton had quite accurately foreseen that the
quarrel of his irascible young principal with
Rapsey was one which it would be well to
adjust, and that no good would come of it.

When the news of the meeting between
Bryceson and Shelman reached his ears, the
cashier was supplied with a reason for the
conduct of Timothy earlier in the day.   There
was a gleam of comfort for him, however, for
it gave him the opportunity of explaining the
circumstances to other customers who might
otherwise have been tempted by rumour to
act in the same manner as others had done.
Towards one or two of the townspeople who
had drawn heavily, Mr. Norton was rather
sharp in his manner when next he met them,
and he had the satisfaction of seeing Messrs.
Beadlemore, Arto, and Follwell presenting
themselves at the Bank to pay in again to
their accounts, and of hearing from Barnabas
Chicklcholt that a knowledge of the real facts
of the case would have prevented the heavy
withdrawals that had alarmed him the day
before.

From the fact that the occurrence was one
for discussion in the Bank itself, it may easily
be supposed that public opinion was pretty
well settled as to the merits of the case.
Shelman had a minority of champions, actuated
chiefly by the fact that his opponent was a
stranger to the town, but on the whole the

verdict of all the informal juries in the place was against him. There had been a rush made for Timothy Rapsey, at once, by the seekers for information, and to a knot of his cronies the little man had imparted all the story. It was received with amazement at first and then with indignation. Be it remembered that the glaziers had but newly finished the renovation of the shattered window-frames, that Avonham men—of the lower orders, it is true, but still Avonham men for all that —were yet in Ridgetown Gaol eating the porridge of affliction for their share of the riot, toiling painfully on the hated treadmill and picking ruefully at the loathsome oakum, for participation in a tumult which the town almost unanimously decided was brought about by the defeated one. It was useless to argue that the commencement of the disturbance, which had everywhere earned for Avonham such an unenviable reputation, a reputation most bitterly resented by its really peaceable inhabitants, was accidental—the scapegoat had been found, and, despite his exalted position in the place, he had many stones flung at him. It would have galled his fiery spirit had he heard those who had been

accustomed to fawn on him now loudest in
their denunciations, and it was well for his
peace of mind that the injuries inflicted on
him by his stalwart conqueror were so severe
as to necessitate strict confinement to his
house, and even to demand medical aid.

During this period of excitement and universal thirst for news and gossip, there was
one person in Avonham who was supremely
uncomfortable. It was fortunate that the
principal portion of Adolphus Carter's work
was mere routine, or assuredly the interests of
his employer would have suffered from the
abstraction and preoccupation of his articled
pupil, who, ordinarily, could be trusted with
important affairs, and who had not in the
least exaggerated his abilities when he had
declared that he was not a fool in his business.
The worst result of his folly that he had
pictured to himself was that Shelman would
have been compelled to eat a little humble-pie
with Timothy Rapsey, and he had not counted,
as indeed his friend had not, on the vigorous
and forcible action of Walter Bryceson being the
first outcome of his confession of his misdeeds
and the share that Shelman had had in them.
From a distance he had witnessed the discomfi-

ture of his associate, and had not dared to move
hand or foot in his service ; and now seated
at his desk he pondered ruefully over the
probable consequences to himself.   He found
no comfort from his meditations ; the more he
thought the matter over the blacker looked
the prospect to him.   To add to his woes, too,
every one of the callers at Mr. Bompas's office
seemed to imagine that he took the liveliest
interest in the affray, and plied him with
awkward questions and distasteful chatter.
Perhaps the one slender piece of consolation
which came to him was the thought that
Shelman had met the punishment with which
he had threatened *him* in his irritation.   But
it was scanty consolation, after all, and there
was no man in Avonham that day with
thoughts more bitter, and prospects more
gloomy, than Adolphus Carter.

It took him a long time to make up his
mind to visit the defeated man, and it was
more through fear of incurring his anger
than from sympathy with him that he at last
determined to do so.   He quitted the office
ostensibly for dinner, and made his way
down the bustling and busy street, giving the
briefest returns to the various greetings he

received. The man who opened the door to him, Shelman's own servant, looked doubtful when he asked to see his master.

"Master's very ill, sir," he said hesitatingly, adding after a pause, "I suppose you know, sir?"

Carter nodded.

"I'll take your name up, Mr. Carter, and see if master will see you," said the man.

Carter waited the man's return with some trepidation. In a minute he came downstairs and asked Carter to walk up.

"Is he in bed?" Adolphus asked, as he prepared to mount the stairs.

"No, sir," answered the man, "he's in his room, sir, but he is sitting up. Doctor Mompesson wanted him to remain in bed, but master was obstinate and would get up. We've had an awful time with him, sir," he added, lowering his voice to a confidential whisper, "there's no pleasing him or doing anything right for him. I hope you've brought no news to upset him, sir?"

This intelligence was the reverse of sooth-ing to Adolphus's already agitated nerves, and he ascended to his friend's bedroom with a hearty inward wish that he had never thought of coming.

Alfred Shelman was not a pretty sight to look at, certainly. His forehead was swollen and discoloured, his eyes were almost closed, and there was a cut under one of them ; his nose was as red as a beet-root, and his lips thrice their usual thickness ; there was a long strip of plaster crossed with smaller slips, where the back of his head had come in contact with the stones ; where no marks were visible his face was deadly pale, and his trembling hands proved that the shock to his system had been severe. No one would have doubted the physical courage with which he had faced his opponent after seeing the terrible results of the battle. Adolphus was seized with new terrors as he reflected on what might have been his lot on the night of the election, and what Fate might yet have in store for him.

" My dear fellow," he said, advancing and holding out his hand in token of sympathy, " I am awfully sorry to see you like this."

" Are you ? " said Shelman, without taking the proffered hand ; " you ought to be. Now perhaps you will be satisfied, when you see the result of your cursed folly."

He spoke with difficulty and indeed with pain, but even then his pallid face flushed with rage, and the distortion of his features gave him so evil an appearance that Carter felt inclined to flee.

He stood his ground, however, and commenced his exculpation.

"I can't really see," he began, "how I am to blame ; I would have suffered anything, I am sure, to have prevented it."

"I wish you had to suffer this !" said Shelman fiercely, striking his head, though he winced and groaned from the pain the hasty action caused him ; "but I'll be revenged on the pair of you when I get about again. If there is any law in the land, that brawling bully shall suffer its penalties, and you may look to yourself, Adolphus Carter, for I will be even with you for your share in the affair, trust me !"

"I declare," said Adolphus earnestly, "upon my most sacred word of honour——"

"*Your* sacred word of honour," said Shelman with a sneer. "That will be a precious guarantee for any asseveration you may be going to make !"

"My word of honour," said Carter, redden-

ing, "was as good as any man's in Avonham
till you and your uncle upset the town with
that cursed election, which has brought us
both into trouble ; and then, if it had not been
for our personal spite against those two, we
should not have had anything worse than the
regret of defeat. I don't defend myself, but
it is not very generous of you to throw all
the blame upon me. I have suffered quite
as much as you have, though in a different
way. You're not just, Shelman."

" It's your turn to triumph over me now,"
said Shelman, viciously, " but you wait for
my turn ! Whether I'm just or not, I'll let
you know my power, at any rate."

" I have not the least desire to triumph
over you," said Carter ; " you are very wrong
in thinking so ; and as for your revenge, your
sentiments on that head are positively wicked."

" Are you going to preach me a sermon,
you hypocrite ? " snarled Shelman.

" No, I am not," answered Adolphus.
" Perhaps you think that you are to be
allowed to threaten and bully without meeting any retort or defence ; do you expect that
I shall permit you to injure me without my
retaliating ? Don't you drive to desperation

a man who has been already driven hard enough and far enough, through carrying out your dirty plans."

Shelman's features became perfectly fiendish with passion. He rose from the armchair in which he was sitting, and made a half-step towards Carter, who prepared for an attack. The effort was, however, too much for him, and he sank back with a groan of pain. For a minute or two he passed his hand over his forehead, whilst Adolphus stood watching him with a face full of alarm, and, to do him justice, of sympathy.

"You are ill," he said at last—"let me get you some brandy or something; can you tell me where it is?"

Shelman's physical pain conquered his rage for a time; he pointed to a cupboard, from which Carter took some brandy and gave him some, mixed with water.

"I won't agitate you by any more talk," said he, when he had rendered him this service; "I really did not come here to quarrel or to blame you; my only object was to see how you were."

"Well," said Shelman faintly, but with no abatement of his malice, "now you have seen

—and feasted your eyes on my condition—you can go."

"I am going," said Carter, taking his hat from the table, "but before I do go I will say one thing——"

"Say it quickly and go then," said Shelman.

"You are very foolish to quarrel with me," said Carter impressively, turning as he spoke, "for I verily believe that I am the only friend you have in Avonham at the present minute."

His hand was on the handle of the door, and he was going, when Shelman cried out hoarsely, "Stop! come here, come back; sit down and wait a minute while I recover a little." Adolphus turned back and sat down; Shelman struggled with himself, and drank a little more of the brandy and water.

"Tell me," he said, "what they are saying about this affair in the town. I suppose the whole place is full of it?"

Mr. Carter owned that it had been the chief topic of conversation that day.

"Curse the cackling fools! what are they saying about it?"

"They put it down to the election and the attack on the 'Coombes,'" answered Carter;

" of course, you know, Timothy Rapsey has been talking."

" Has he said anything against the Bank ?" said Shelman eagerly, " has he done that ?"

" I don't know that he has," said Carter, " I haven't been near the little brute all day —I only know what has passed from conversations I have had with people in the office."

" Find out, will you ?" said Shelman ; " get to know all that he has said, speak to him yourself ; don't frighten him, but get out of him all you can and let me know to-morrow. Hush ! here is someone coming upstairs. Don't say a word of this before him, whoever he may be ! "

The servant knocked at the door, and receiving permission to enter, announced Doctor Mompesson, who followed immediately on his heels.

The doctor gave a glance of displeasure at the visitor, and shook his finger reproachingly at the patient.

" This won't do, Shelman, you know ; I must forbid you to see any visitors for a day or two."

" I was so confoundedly hipped here all alone, doctor," said Shelman, taking the excuse out of Carter's mouth, "that when Carter called I ordered him to be shown up."

"I haven't been here ten minutes, Doctor," said Carter, and extending his hand to his unfortunate friend, who, this time, did not refuse it, he backed out of the room. Outside the house he waited for the doctor, who made his appearance in about a quarter of an hour. He was not driving, so Carter joined him, and they walked townwards together.

"What do you think of him?" he asked.

"What do you?" said the doctor drily.

"I think he looks very bad," said Carter.

"He *is* very bad," said Doctor Mompesson, "and your visit hasn't done him any good; I have given strict injunctions that no one is to be admitted to see him yet, not even his uncle."

"I didn't think I was doing any harm by calling," said Carter, penitently; "of course I was naturally anxious to know how he was getting on."

"Naturally," answered the doctor, "but he must be kept in perfect quietness."

"I suppose," said Adolphus, hesitatingly, "he has been—been soundly—I mean very severely injured!"

"He has been handled about as roughly as ever a man was," answered Doctor Mompesson gravely. "Before you were born, Mr. Adolphus, and when I was a younger man, I attended a good many prize-fights — it was more the fashion then—and I don't think I can remember the case of a man receiving such an amount of punishment in so short a space of time. If you have any difference with Mr. Bryceson, don't attempt to settle it *that* way, young fellow, I advise you."

Adolphus, recollecting how narrowly he had escaped the same treatment, experienced the sensation quaintly described as that of "a person walking over his grave."

"Is he in any danger?" he asked after walking on silently for half a minute.

"No immediate danger," said the doctor, "so long as he is kept perfectly quiet, as I told you, and that is why I have put the veto on any callers. *Encephalitis* is what I'm most afraid of," he added, half to himself and half to Carter, "but we can avoid that with care, I think."

Adolphus had not the slightest idea of what *encephalitis* might be, and was somewhat alarmed at the idea that his confederate was in danger of an ailment with so formidable a name.

"I hope he will soon recover," he said, and really meant it too.

"I hope so," answered the doctor, "for his own sake and for other people's as well."

And with these parting words, which bore no grain of consolation to Adolphus, the doctor bade him good-day and crossed the road to call on an old friend who would be treated by no one else, although, as we have before said, Doctor Mompesson had practically retired from his profession.

Adolphus turned moodily into South Street, but brightened up as he saw Timothy Rapsey on the other side of the way. For a moment he forgot Shelman's advice not to frighten him, and determined that he should share the unpleasant feelings under which he himself was suffering. He crossed the road and accosted the little man.

"This is a bad business about Shelman," he commenced, carefully watching Timothy's face.

"Ah!" said Timothy, looking wise, "perhaps it will teach Mr. Shelman a lesson, Mr. Carter."

"I'm afraid it will teach some one else a lesson," answered Carter, lugubriously. "I wouldn't be in your shoes if he were to die, Rapsey; you set Mr. Bryceson on to him, you know. It's your fault from beginning to end, and I only hope you won't have precious good cause to remember it."

"But," stammered Timothy, not attempting to protest his guiltlessness in the matter, but dreadfully alarmed by this speech, "Mr. Shelman isn't in any *danger*, is he?"

"*Isn't* he?" said Carter, nodding his head in the emphatic manner which generally accompanies this question when put sarcastically.

"No, but *is* he?" said Timothy, much alarmed, he scarcely knew at what; "you talked about his dying, Mr. Carter—he's not going to *die*, you know."

"*Isn't* he?" said Adolphus, nodding again in the same manner. "I don't know anything about it; all I know is that he's got something I can't pronounce, and that Doctor Mompesson is very doubtful how the case will end, and I wish you joy of your interference, Mr. Rapsey!"

So saying, Adolphus Carter flung himself

into his office, leaving Timothy, much disturbed, to wend his way towards the market-place, shaking his head very solemnly over the mysterious disease that Mr. Carter could not pronounce, and wondering how long it took to kill a patient suffering from it. Mr. Rapsey was so ill at ease that he did not, as usual, join the busy throng in the streets, but retired to his own quarters, where he passed the afternoon reading a large illustrated edition of the " Death of Abel." He met Edward in the evening, and confided to him what he had heard of Shelman's condition.

" It jes' sarves Mas'r Shelman right," said the negro. " In de fus' place, dar warn't de leas' 'scuse for 'um int'ferin' wid our haouse or de people in it. An', in de secon' place. Mas'r Rapsey, a feller 'at's got a head like a bun ain't got no bizness goin' fightin'."

CHAPTER X.

VERY demure looked the young ladies of the
Bompas family on their return to Avonham,
a week after the events last narrated. The
only outward signs of their London visit were
some sweet novelties in Regent Street dresses
and Bond Street bonnets, which so far as the
female portions of his congregation was concerned, completely nullified any of the preach-
ing of the good old vicar, on the first Sunday
after their arrival, and caused many Avonham
young ladies to give way to outbursts of semi-
hysterical satire, and many matrons to thank
Heaven that their daughters were not as other
men's were. The young ladies themselves
were soon the recipients of feminine congratulations couched in various shades of envy,
hatred, and malice, but to them, who could,
as we have observed, take their own part in
this phase of feminine warfare remarkably
well, these gave but little concern. They
were perfectly prepared for the satire, whereas

the resident maidens had not counted on the bonnets.

Those who hastened to pour into the ears of the worthy father of our fair friends the thrilling history of the latest battle of Avonham were a little disappointed at finding that their news was stale. They were met on the threshold of their story by the information that the whole facts of the case were well known to him. Never suspecting the source from which he had obtained his knowledge—for, like most inquisitive people, they were unable to perceive the facts that lay under their very noses—they imagined that Mr. Bompas had been made acquainted with all that had passed in Avonham during his absence, from correspondence with his friends and his office. They were also disappointed at getting no opinion from him upon the subject, beyond the broad statement that it was a pity for young men to quarrel, that a personal encounter was at all times a matter for regret and a thing to be deplored by the friends of both parties, that the whole affair appeared to be the result of injudicious chatter, and that he, for one, declined to commit himself to any other expression of opinion about it.

Mr. Bompas oracularly delivered this opinion at the first meeting of the Club which he attended after his return from London, and his ideas being warmly supported by Mr. Sennett, and by peace-loving Reuben Matley, who possessed that influence which a uniformly quiet man of parts always has in a country town, the matter, after a good deal of cogitation on the part of those who had made it the leading topic for a week, became unpopular and began to lose interest in Avonham.

During the period of Mr. Bompas's stay in London, the town had been deprived of the presence of three more of its shining lights. Mrs. Stanhope had been absent and Sir Headingly Cann had been seeking relaxation from his labours. Mr. Boldham had likewise withdrawn the light of his countenance for awhile, and therefore the interest of the town was considerably whetted when, within a few days of each other, all these notabilities returned to Avonham. Old inhabitants began to think that life in Marlshire was exciting for aged nerves, and the middle-aged and young natives would have, at this time, repudiated with scorn any insinuation that the place could, with any fairness, be described as dull.

Mrs. Stanhope returned for the purpose of setting her house in order before her marriage. She was going also to give another of her receptions to the county magnates, and wished her last independent fixture to be a success. It had been agreed between the various parties interested in the forthcoming marriage, that no announcement of it should be permitted to tickle the ears of the Avonham folk just yet. There was no intention of concealing the ceremony when it did take place ; on the contrary, it was determined that all Avonham should be gay that day, and that the affair should be as brilliant as possible.

Sir Headingly Cann had returned for the purpose of overhauling and tautening such portions of the political rigging of the good ship Britannia as were entrusted to his care. He had to meet his constituents, to congratulate them on the fact that the country, which had been in such deadly peril whilst the opposite party had been the Ins, was now saved by the fact that the opposite party were now the Outs. He also felt that, after the late contest, it behoved him to keep a careful watch over the town, so as to be able to hand over the political succession to his nephew, when the time came, unfettered by the unpleasant conditions of a hard-fought election.

Walter Rivers accompanied Sir Headingly, and was on the most excellent terms with himself and the whole world. His suit was prosperous, as it could not fail to be if there were any sense of gratitude in woman, for the young fellow left no stone unturned to please and gratify the mistress of his heart. Anything like youthful sentiment would have been thrown away on a woman of the strength of mind and force of character of Mrs. Stanhope, and Rivers was not so shallow or so short-sighted as to attempt it. But there are other forms of adoration, more suitable for a woman who confesses to having passed thirty-five, and confesses it without making any bones about it ; and Walter Rivers was quite man of the world enough to know them. So it followed that the course of this particular true love commenced smoothly and fairly enough, however it might be destined to end.

Mr. Boldham came back to see how much mischief his nephew had done in his absence, and to endeavour to patch up matters as best he could. His was no congenial task but a most difficult one, for, setting aside the temporary scare about the Bank, at which he could afford to laugh, the mismanagement of Shelman occurring just at the time when he was making his bow to the world as a politician was vastly embarrassing to the ambitious man, whom it injured most of all.

To Timothy Rapsey's great relief, Alfred Shelman did not succumb to the unpronounceable disease, and a few days after his uncle's arrival was again about in the town. What had passed between him and Mr. Boldham no one knew, but it was surmised that it was not a pleasant meeting for either of them. Those who knew anything of the affairs of the Bank were aware that it was impossible that Shelman's position could be assailed by his uncle, that he held too much influence and had too much capital in the concern to be treated even as an ordinary partner, and it was whispered among a chosen and select few that at the interview the younger man had more than held his own against the elder.

The inhabitants of the " Coombes " went on much as usual. It was a matter of great wonderment to some of the townspeople as to who was the real owner of the house, for Bryceson seemed as much at home in it as Galbraith had been, and Fred Markham speedily occupied in the place the position previously filled by Bryceson. There appeared to be a good deal of cordial intercourse between the two young men and Mr. Bompas's family, and Mr. Millard seemed to be on excellent terms at the house, which had been exalted into a veritable Aladdin's palace of wonders by the graphic descriptions given of the interior by Mr. Rapsey.

Two conversations which took place a few days after Mrs. Stanhope's return would perhaps have caused as much wonder if both had been heard, as the display of a roc's egg on the roof of the " Coombes " would have done. It was a fine morning, and Bryceson and Markham mounted their horses for a visit to Beytesbury, where old Millard had offered them some shooting. Crossing the market-place slowly, they came upon the carriage of Mrs. Stanhope standing, as on another occasion which we have noticed, at the door of Mr. Pollimoy's shop. Mrs. Stanhope had left the carriage and was in the shop, waited on as before by Traveller Pollimoy. Mr. Fred Markham dismounted and entered.

" I want a pocket-book, if you please," said he to Miss Ruth Pollimoy.

Miss Pollimoy went to the back of the shop to get the desired article. Fred stood with his back to the counter for the two minutes which she occupied in her search, and looked round the shop ; Mrs. Stanhope, seated sideways at the opposite counter, looked across at him and noticed two things—one that he was an uncommonly handsome young man, the other that he was glancing at her in a manner which she construed to be one of admiration. She was not displeased, she was accustomed to being admired ; there was nothing bold in the glance either, and the man was evidently a gentleman.

There was very little difficulty about the selection of the pocket-book ; Markham handled two or three, chose one, paid for it, left the shop, and mounted his horse.

" Who is that ? " asked the Queen of Avonham, as he rode away.

" I don't know the gentleman's name, madam," said Mr. Pollimoy, " but he is staying with Mr. Bryceson, the gentleman on the other horse, at Mr. Galbraith's house, the one that he purchased of you, madam."

" Indeed," said Mrs. Stanhope, carelessly.

" Yes, madam," said Pollimoy, " he has not

been here long, indeed he only arrived on the day "—here he gave a little cough—" previous to the—the unfortunate encounter between Mr. Shelman and Mr. Bryceson—of which I daresay, madam, you have heard."

" I have heard of it," said Mrs. Stanhope.

" A very deplorable circumstance," ventured Mr. Pollimoy, quoting Mr. Bompas at the Club.

" In one way, certainly," said Mrs. Stanhope, rising and unclasping her purse to pay the bill which Mr. Pollimoy had deferentially laid before her, " but as Mr. Shelman never loses an opportunity of making himself excessively disagreeable and obnoxious to every one around him, it is perhaps a very good thing that he has found someone in Avonham with spirit enough to refuse to submit to his arrogance, and ability to give him a punishment which he has thoroughly deserved for a long time past. I am only sorry it was not done before, and sincerely glad that it has been done now."

Mr. Pollimoy's astonishment fairly overcame his obsequiousness ; he returned Mrs. Stanhope her change with a wild stare, and without a word of thanks, and completely forgot to execute his little run round his counter to the

door, and thence to the carriage, as his patron
went away. For the first time Mrs. Stanhope
went out of the stationer's shop unattended,
and she left the proprietor staring at his
daughter in a feeble and foolish manner, and
with thoughts almost too deep for expression
in words.

"Ruth, my dear," he said solemnly, "did
you hear what Mrs. Stanhope said ? "

"Yes, papa."

"Did you ever hear anything more astonish-
ing in your life, Ruth ? "

"Well, yes, papa, I have. I am not so
much astonished as you seem to be."

"You are not so much astonished as I seem
to be," repeated Mr. Pollimoy slowly ; "and
pray why are you not so much astonished as I
seem to be ? as I *am*, indeed ? "

"Perhaps," said Ruth Pollimoy, laughing—
she was a merry girl, with more than the
average Avonham sense of humour—"perhaps
I could answer your question better if you told
me what there is in Mrs. Stanhope's last
speech that causes you so much astonishment."

"My dear," said Mr. Pollimoy, "I don't
know what you have thought of it, but it has
been my idea, and the idea, too, of a great

many people who have more reason to know
than I have, that if there was a likely match
in Avonham, it was Mrs. Stanhope and Mr.
Alfred Shelman. Do you wonder at my feeling astonished ? "

" Not under those circumstances, papa,"
answered Miss Ruth, " but you were completely wrong about Mrs. Stanhope and Mr.
Shelman. I never thought that would come
to anything."

" Didn't you, my dear ? "

" Oh dear no," said Ruth, laughing and
shaking her pretty curls, " and I'm very glad
for Mrs. Stanhope's sake that it isn't so, for
my opinion of Mr. Shelman is precisely the
same as hers is."

" Well, my dear, it is not my place to say
anything against Mr. Shelman, but I must
say he has an unpopular manner with him.
Nevertheless with respect to Mrs. Stanhope's
words about him, I have never been more astonished in all my life. No," he added reflectively, out of the depths of his vast experience
of the world, " not in the course of all my
travels have I been more surprised."

Perhaps Mrs. Stanhope had calculated on
leaving some such astonishment behind her,

and had reckoned on the fact that her opinion
of the man whose name had once been coupled
with hers, and whom she had so decisively
rejected, would, in gossiping Avonham, be
brought to his ears, for the leader of Avonham
society was not in the habit of taking her
tradesmen into her confidence.

When Markham had emerged from the shop,
and had mounted, the friends rode on together
until they were clear of the town, and out of
hearing of anyone. Then Bryceson, checking
his horse, said :

" Well ? "

" Well, I never had the slightest doubt of
the matter in my own mind, after Harry described to me the way he had followed on her
track, but it's some satisfaction to have seen
her for myself," said Markham.

" There is no doubt at all, I suppose ? "
asked Bryceson earnestly, and with emphasis.

" There is not the shadow of a doubt,"
answered Markham, " I will swear it is the
same woman ! "

" Has she altered much ? "

" Less than you would fancy ; she is state-
lier and looks quieter, and on the whole has
improved vastly in her appearance. Tom

Reynolds knew her a good deal better than any of Reginald's friends, for Tom was always round at Reggie's house. Of course you and Harry were at college then ; Tom used often to tell me that she would never rest easy unless she had every man in the room dancing attendance and making open love to her. It used to drive Reginald mad, poor fellow ! and I expect there were words about it when they were alone, and that led to the other affair. I don't know whether she meant any harm at first, but I suppose it's confoundedly hard for a woman like that to pull up when once she commences to take the down-hill road."

"How do you account," said Bryceson, when they had ridden a little farther, "for a wild bird like that settling down comfortably and contentedly in this sleepy old hencoop ? "

"Women are strange animals," was the only solution to the problem that Fred Markham could find.

"I shall be glad to see Harry back," said Bryceson, "for if anything should take place in his absence that made it necessary for matters to be brought to a head, I should find myself in the unpleasant position of setting the town on fire for the second time."

"Yes, Avonham will have something to talk about if there is any exposure; you'll make a heroic figure jumping up in church and forbidding the banns, if Harry's surmise is correct and the dear creature thinks of venturing her neck in the matrimonial noose for the third time. Well, I'll stand by you, old boy, and, mind you, we hold a very strong hand in the game."

"And that, and the knowledge that I'm serving Harry and Reginald, are my only consolations, I assure you."

With that, the conversation dropped, and the two friends were soon busily engaged in discussing the capital lunch which Mrs. Millard set before the young men, prior to their making havoc among her husband's partridges.

Mr. Pollimoy was not chary of imparting the news of Mrs. Stanhope's comments on the late affray to his cronies; and her opinion was not long in reaching Mr. Alfred Shelman's ears. The lines of this young man were not, just now, cast in pleasant places. Baulked of obtaining the widow's hand, made the object of her open satire and scorn, thrashed like a dog in the open market-place, terrified by the probability of being made an accessory to the riot, and conscious that, without possessing the power of retaliation, he was the theme of all the idle chatter of the town, it is certain that for whomsoever the current of life was flowing smoothly, it was the reverse of placid for him.

To Walter Rivers, on the other hand, everything seemed to be going well. A handsome and wealthy bride, a parliamentary career, which he felt would be an honourable one, riches and influence were all at his feet. He regarded both his past and his future with complacency, regretting little in the former, fearing nothing in the latter; and yet both he and his affianced wife, whilst dreaming that they were simply floating down a limpid stream, that led with easy gliding to happiness and fame, were being imperceptibly swept along on a treacherous river that had hidden rocks and deadly depths, and led from peaceful scenes and tranquil places to the roaring and destroying ocean.

END OF VOL. II.